An Elf's

The Golden

Book T

By

Laurie Cook

An Elf's Sacrifice

The Goldenfell Saga
Book Three

PUBLISHED BY PLP PUBLICATIONS

FEBRUARY 2024

PROLOGUE

Another season had come and again there had been no word from the Queen! He had received messages from others in her name, biding him to patience, but he was still awaiting final instructions. Time for him was running out! The speculation was starting again. If he did not leave soon, he would be discovered.

The River Lord gazed out at the water that flowed by his fortress. The lizard-man threat had disappeared abruptly and now his fortresses on this side of the river were largely redundant. Only those on the other side were needed for defense and they had not been called upon for years. At least on this side of the river he was closer to where he needed to be.

The River Lord! Why had he ever agreed to use that stupid name? Instead of being here and leading these Men of the forts, he should have been at home. He had lamented his decision not to respond to the Call when it had first been issued but he had ignored it and all that it meant. Now it might be too late, and all his sorrow could never change that!

CHAPTER ONE

When Thomaline's huge grey mountain cat and beloved pet rushed through the corridor, away from the royal chambers, Brandt should have wondered at Alred's hurried departure. He had, however, continued on his way, unaware of a problem until he reached the doors of their apartment. Once there, Alred's defection, combined with the pained looks on the faces of the two guards that stood at attention on either side of those doors finally forced Brandt to acknowledge that something was amiss. The act that finally set off a warning bell in his head was the crash of something striking the inside wall of their chambers. The noise brought him to a sudden and complete stop.

"What's going on?" he asked the guards, but both elves merely shook their heads in their attempt at deniability as they remained at stoic attention, intent on their duty. Brand moved cautiously to the door and listened carefully before advancing further. It sounded like Thomaline's voice, but he could honestly say that he had rarely heard her sound so angry. Who was in there and the recipient of that anger? Another crash, this time on the other side of the door directly in front of Brandt, made him back up and re-evaluate whether he really needed to enter their apartment. The guards refused to look at him, keeping their gaze on the wall, directly in front of them.

"Who's in there with the Queen?"

"We have seen no one else enter, My Lord."

"Is she alone then?" he asked the pair as something else crashed into the door.

"I believe so, My Lord. The Queen only returned a short time before you arrived," one of the guards volunteered.

Thomaline's actions must then have something to do with the prince and princess of the Skellan Elves, Brandt reasoned. Not even Skith, the head of

Thomaline's Council, had ever caused her to release this much rage. Carefully, he opened the door and peered around the edge. A wine goblet very narrowly missed his nose, but he jumped through the doorway, hands raised in surrender, before any other missiles could be launched.

"Thomaline! It's me!" he shouted as he quickly took in the scene and noticed that Thomaline had her arm cocked for another throw. "What's wrong?"

The answer was immediate and profane, but the goblet that was clutched in her hand remained where it was. In all their eighty years together, he had rarely heard Thomaline swear and then, never more than mildly. Now, he found himself surprised at her imagination and variety and that was even before she reverted to an old Elvish dialect instead of the common tongue in which she had previously been so eloquent. Brandt found himself reminded of the fact that she had spent several hundred years in the company of rough soldiers and some of that language had clearly been remembered. Maybe even improved upon! He did not understand much of what she was saying at present, but it was clear that her anger was in no way diminished. Deciding that further questions could wait until she was calmer, Brandt righted one of the chairs that had been overturned and sat down. It took a few minutes, but Thomaline finally seemed to run out of verbal steam although she continued to stride around the room. The unfortunate wine goblet had not remained in her hand for long and now lay with others on the floor.

"Feeling better?"

"No! Not at all! I still want to destroy something!" Thomaline raked her loose, long golden blonde hair back from her beautiful face with one hand while the other remained fisted at her side.

"Would you like a glass of wine after all that shouting? If you haven't broken the bottle, that is."

"It is not amusing Brandt! Those two are driving me mad!"

His suspicions confirmed, Brandt just nodded in sympathy and agreement and rose to check the sideboard for the wine. Miraculously, the bottle was still there, untouched. He picked it up and poured some wine into the one remaining goblet before he turned to Thomaline. "Here. Have a little of this. It might make you feel better."

Thomaline huffed at that idea but accepted the wine nonetheless and then moved to sit in the chair that Brandt had just vacated. He, meanwhile, began to search for another goblet that might look as if it could still hold some liquid. After successfully finding one hiding under an overturned chair, Brandt poured his own drink after setting the chair back on its legs.

"What happened this time?"

Instead of answering, or even taking a drink from her goblet, Thomaline sat brooding. Never a fool, Brandt decided to let her take her time. It must be something very bad; he thought. Thomaline had a temper, but it had usually been contained with icy control no matter how badly she had been provoked. This display of rage and violence was certainly unusual and did not bode well for anyone, especially him.

Thomaline glared into her goblet, but still did not take a drink. After a moment more, she passed it over to Brandt.

"Take this. I do not want wine right now." As Brandt took the goblet from Thomaline's hand, she rose and began pacing the room once more. "They are not happy with their situation! They feel that I have not been fair! They are seeking more concessions! He keeps complaining that he has no yaral. She keeps 'suggesting' that I should seek her guidance as she seems to think she has 'experience' that I lack. It goes on and on! And he still hints that I need a king, not a consort!" 'They' of course, were the prince and princess of the Skellan Elves. The twin rulers of Goldenfell's former enemies.

Brandt nodded but did not interrupt even though the thought that the prince was still conniving to replace him set his blood to boil.

Eighty years before, when Thomaline and Brandt had made the long journey from his land to her homeland of Goldenfell, it was to find the land and its people leaderless and under assault by foreign elves. The enemy elves were the Skellan, a race of elves from another land and through treachery, their king had betrayed and murdered Thomaline's uncle, the former King Leyrd. Thomaline's return had barely been in time to help fend off their attack and to establish the Ward of protection created by Leyrd, that was to keep all the land of Goldenfell safe from any outside threat. As the Ward had been created by the king, it required someone from the royal bloodline to initialize its power and Thomaline was the last of that line. Unfortunately, the Ward had not been completely successful. An error in Leyrd's calculations had made the

Ward unstable and two years previously, it had been in imminent danger of complete failure. The timing could not have been worse. While the Ward had protected the Goldenfell Elven lands, it also had prevented them from learning what was happening outside their realm. Because of this, an unforeseen threat had gathered on the edges of Goldenfell's borders, waiting for their chance to overrun and destroy the Elves of Goldenfell. They were the Xarlerii; a lizard-like creature that had earlier driven the Skellan Elves from their own homeland and into the lands of Goldenfell. While Goldenfell had been relatively safe behind the protection of their Ward, the Skellan had been entrenched in the mountains to the north of Thomaline's kingdom, trying to hang on to a life in a new land while still dealing with the Xarlerii menace.

The Xarlerii had followed the defeated Skellan Elves as they retreated to the new land of Goldenfell, and the Xarlerii swarm had quickly increased their numbers until they once again threatened to destroy the refugee elves. Fortunately, before the Ward of Goldenfell was completely spent, Thomaline had sent out scouts to learn what had transpired in the outside world during the time that the kingdom had been hidden away. The news that had been gathered was alarming. The scouts brought back information regarding the Xarlerii threat, and they also brought word from the Skellan Elves. As opposed to the Xarlerii, the Skellan had been reduced in numbers by the many years of continued conflict with their enemy and they had been forced to make a last stand in the northern mountains. After learning of the Xarlerii threat, Thomaline made the decision to offer the remaining Skellan sanctuary within the lands of Goldenfell, in exchange for information and their help in fighting the Xarlerii. The prince and princess were the new rulers and much regretted their predecessor's cowardly attack against Goldenfell. They had been more than grateful to accept Thomaline's offer, and all their people were moved to the fortress of Goldenspire while the remaining fighting force of Skellan soldiers, led by Prince Cathos, joined with Thomaline's army. Following a successful battle, a new Ward had been established, and as all the elves felt safe once more, the mingling of the two former enemies had looked promising. At least for a while.

When the remaining Skellan had made their way to Goldenspire, accommodations had been hastily constructed, but these new quarters had been a vast improvement over the conditions in which the Skellan had been living in the mountains. The efforts of the inhabitants of Goldenfell had been appreciated by the weary refugees. Despite being offered quarters in the fortress, Princess Agretha had been insistent regarding her wish to remain with her people while Thomaline, Brandt and the combined army rode to war. Their victory over the Xarlerii had come at a cost of many lives and even Thomaline and Brandt had been injured, but their success had safely secured the land of Goldenfell and upon the return of the army, life had settled into a new rhythm with the Skellan Elves offered full integration into Goldenfell society. New friendships had been established and romance had followed for some. Even Thomaline's cold and austere Head of Council had not been immune. Skith's relationship with Princess Agretha had been seen as a beacon of promise for all and more affairs of the heart had followed. Unfortunately, before too long that promising start had started to wane.

Prince Cathos had been the instigator of much of the disharmony. Before the prince had been invited to live in Goldenfell, one of Thomaline's former councilors had secretly gone to the Skellan and tricked Prince Cathos into thinking that Thomaline was in need of a strong candidate for king. Cathos had not known that the councilor Mendeth no longer represented Thomaline, and the prince had made a blunder or two before being firmly set straight by Thomaline and Brandt. The prince had apologized for his mistake and seemed to have put the matter behind him, but it was not long after the battle with the Xarlerii that Cathos's thoughts returned to the matter of kingship. Although he did his poor best to hide his feelings, Prince Cathos was appalled by the idea that Brandt was Thomaline's choice of Consort. He could not believe that a Man with only a smidgeon of Elven blood had been granted that position to the greatest treasure of the land! He had begun a campaign that to his mind, would help Thomaline see the error of her ways. His ego was massive and while Cathos might have thought he was being subtle; his aim was very apparent to Thomaline. He wanted to be Thomaline's king and Brandt did not doubt that the Prince would keep up his campaign, despite his general air of magnanimous ineptitude. Brandt clearly remembered that Cathos had proved himself to be a capable warrior in the battle against the Xarlerii.

In the beginning, the prince had seemingly adjusted well to life in Goldenfell, but that was before he managed to sow strife amongst many in Goldenfell's court. It had started with the Lady Sullan. Sullan was one of

Thomaline newest councilors and almost as young as Thomaline herself. Sullan was certainly not accustomed to the attention of someone like Prince Cathos as even Thomaline had to admit that he could be quite charming when it suited him. Over that fall and winter, he had made it his mission to court the lovely Lady Sullan and at first, he must have been quite sincere. Sullan had one major ability which no one, outside of Thomaline, Brandt and key councilors, knew. Sullan had the ability to detect lies. She knew when someone was not being truthful, and she had used this ability diligently when the Skellan had first arrived in Goldenspire to ensure that all was as it seemed. It was this ability that had allowed Thomaline to place as much trust as she had in the Skellan Elves when they had agreed to move to Goldenspire and to help in the battle against the Xarlerii. In the beginning, Sullan had been totally enraptured with the prince, just as Skith had been with his sister, the princess. Prince Cathos's eventual defection had left the Lady Sullan heartbroken, and the kernel of unhappiness and dissatisfaction sown by the prince began to spread to others.

Prince Cathos then turned his attentions to another and then another, but all the while he played to Thomaline as if she should be jealous of his affairs. Unfortunately, Prince Cathos's high opinion of himself was not shared by others, especially Thomaline and certainly not Brandt. Brandt spent more than a few idle hours wondering how and where he could dispose of the body if the prince's unwanted attentions towards Thomaline did not cease. Brandt knew he could more than look after himself in a fight, fair or otherwise and was often amused at the blatant attempts by the prince to discredit him, but Brandt felt the unorthodox and unwanted pursuit was something with which Thomaline should not have to contend. The prince was either an overconfident fool or secretly working on some other agenda. Brandt was almost willing to bet that the prince was a fool but was not about to underestimate him. It was unfortunate that Cathos had no real duties with which to keep himself occupied. It would have been better for them all if the prince had spent more time seeing to the needs of his people, but he had been leaving most of that duty to Thomaline and his sister.

In the wake of Prince Cathos's romantic chaos, Skith's continued relationship with Princess Agretha had also become increasingly strained by her changing moods and demands, even though the Chief Councilor acceded to more 'requests' than Thomaline would have liked. Grumblings by the pair had caused accommodations for the prince and princess to be upgraded and they were now ensconced in their own apartments within Goldenspire. Those rooms were on the other side of the fortress and although Thomaline and Brandt's quarters were firmly off limits, occasionally the prince seemed to have become confused as to the location of his own rooms and he had been escorted from the Queen's area more than once.

"Dare I ask what they're seeking now?"

"She does not like their quarters and keeps asking for a role here in Goldenspire. If she were to ask more for her people, I might have more respect for Agretha, but she seems to want to have her say over my subjects. When they first arrived in Goldenspire, all her concern was for her own people. Now, she seems to have abandoned that sentiment to concentrate solely on her own well-being. When she is not pointing out my deficiencies as a ruler that is, and he is just as bad. I cannot allow him any real duties because of his careless attitude and his ambition. He is still upset that no yaral will take to him or his soldiers. Somehow, he thinks it is my doing. He also does not understand why they have been forbidden access to certain areas of Goldenspire. He wonders what it is that we must be hiding from them." Thomaline was still agitated and began to pace the room once more.

"The only thing hiding is any good sense that either of them previously possessed!" Brandt was starting to share Thomaline's anger, although he had to admit that the prince was right about one thing. They were indeed hiding something. The orb that housed the Ward of Goldenfell was kept and guarded in the Royal quarters, but only a few select individuals were entrusted with the knowledge of its whereabouts.

As to the yaral, Brandt could certainly see why none would put up with the prince, but why they had not engaged with any of the Skellan soldiers was a mystery to him.

The yaral had been introduced to Goldenspire by Thomaline. When she and Brandt had made the journey from his land to hers, they had been accompanied by a young wild yaral that Thomaline had found along the way. Yaral were large grey mountain cats. They had dappled markings that helped them blend into the landscape of the mountains. They also had large, tufted ears and huge paws that helped them navigate the snowy mountains. The latest addition to Thomaline's long line of pets had much larger than the original, and since the time of Ari, the first pet yaral, Thomaline had sought out a new cat to bring into their lives with the passing of each animal. A few years earlier, she had established the Queen's Brigade. This was a unit made up of Elven soldiers and some of the wild yaral that had been convinced to come down from the mountains to partner with a soldier of their choice. The idea had been to create an elite fighting unit. Thomaline's current pet Alred, had given her the idea. He was always with Thomaline and Brandt and would defend either of them if needed, but he was indulged as a pet. The new pairing of soldier and yaral worked more as a partnership. The Queen's Brigade had proven very worthy in the fight against the Xarlerii, but their ranks had been decimated in the battle. It had taken the past two years to create a full complement of fighting partners as only a few yaral would agree to the arrangement and they were very picky concerning with whom they would partner. So far, none would have anything to do with any of the Skellan, and especially not Prince Cathos. To a cat, they all seemed to loath the prince. Tallee, the principle Elven animal expert had a theory, but Brandt had not yet learned what Tallee thought the problem might be. He would have to remember to ask him the next time he saw the elf.

"I am not engaging in any further pointless discussions with those two! I have called Skith and the Council along with General Temor to a meeting this afternoon. I am putting an end to this."

"What are you planning?" Brandt asked warily. "I know you're angry, but Thomaline, please don't let that cloud your judgement," he appealed to Thomaline. In her present mood, he could easily foresee something drastic happening to the Skellan leaders.

"Hah! There is nothing clouding my thinking. I have thought about this for a long time, and it is now time to act before any further problems arise or they make even more trouble."

"Are you going to give me a hint?"

Thomaline stopped pacing and stood looking thoughtfully at Brandt. He could see that she had made up her mind as she then moved to sit beside him.

"I am getting rid of them."

"What! You can't! Their people will revolt! Many of them are happy here, even if the prince and princess are not."

"I do not plan to 'get rid' like that. I realize that some are quite content to live among us. What I meant to say is that I am going to offer all the Skellan

Elves an alternative to their unhappiness here in Goldenspire. For those that have issues with my rule, I am going to offer them their own lands."

CHAPTER TWO

Shortly after the noon meal, Thomaline met with her Council and the session was called to order. She wanted to place the matter of removing the Skellan Elves to the others but before she could begin a small disturbance was heard from outside the Council doors.

"I'll see what's happening." Brandt volunteered while the others sat waiting to hear what their Queen had to say.

"We will wait." Thomaline replied and Brandt hurried to the door. He was not surprised by the guard's report. After a few moments, he returned to his chair beside Thomaline.

"It was Prince Cathos. He thought he had been requested to attend our meeting, but the guards advised him otherwise." Brandt stated with a sigh.

A look of anger flashed in Thomaline's eyes, but instead of commenting on the prince's attempted transgression, she gathered her calm and moved forward with her reason for calling the meeting.

"I have called everyone here to discuss a plan that I have been working on and wish to put before you." Thomaline spoke to the seated elves, but her eyes were on Skith. "We have all heard from many of the Skellan Elves in recent months, regarding their unhappiness with living here, in and around Goldenspire." There were murmurings among the councilors; they had all heard complaints of one type or another. "I have been working on a solution and now I would like your input."

"What do you propose, My Queen?" asked Skith, while others very quietly offered a few imaginative suggestions of their own. Brandt had to quickly cover his face with his hand so that no one saw his grin when he overheard Lady Sullan's idea. Thomaline's eyes merely sparkled as she kept the rest of her features carefully neutral. Palin did not even try to contain his grin.

"I realize that most of you have opinions, but please hear what I would like to propose." Thomaline said with a small smile. "We cannot let matters remain the way they are as both the Skellan Elves, and the Elves of Goldenfell are becoming increasingly unhappy with the current situation. I do not want to let matters deteriorate any further. Therefore, I propose that we offer the Skellan and most importantly, their leaders, the opportunity to move to lands of their own. I wish to offer them someplace to set up their own hold and settlements."

The room erupted with excited chatter, and Brandt noticed that most seemed to approve of the idea. Skith, however, was harder to read. The head of the Council had a look of deep contemplation.

"Where do you propose, My Lady? I do not think that there is anywhere near Goldenspire that would be suitable." Skith warily asked.

"In that, you are correct, Skith. It would serve no purpose if they are too near. I am proposing that the Skellan be given lands in the north. I will offer them the area where they used to live." Far enough away from here, she thought.

"My Lady, I doubt that those lands will be very appealing to them. They experienced much hardship there. Surely you will not exile them to that part of the mountains!" Skith exclaimed and Thomaline was not sure if Skith's objections were on behalf of Princess Agretha or just her people.

"That is not my intention Lord Skith. I wish to exile no one or have them suffer as they previously did while trapped in those mountains. What I propose is to help all that wish to leave Goldenspire, begin a new life in an area with which they are already familiar. I do not propose to just send them off, but to assist them with our help, support, and supplies. This way they may create the life they wish. We can supply them with all that they need to set up their own holds once more. In addition, I want to open up a much larger area of the mountains for them and include an area of the plains to encourage them towards self-sufficiency. The Skellan will have their own twin leaders to guide them, and I will not have those two underfoot any longer." She admitted. "They would be able to make their own settlements in either the mountains or the plains, or even both."

Thomaline had given this proposal a lot of thought because of the prince and princess and their recent actions. Many of the Skellan were clearly unhappy and Thomaline dearly wished to have the prince and princess out of her fortress. The pair needed to get back to the business of looking after their own people and establishing a new home for them all should help to accomplish that. There would be some that would not want to move and if the bickering and complaining ceased, Thomaline was happy to have those elves stay. There had been some unions between the two groups that seemed to be quite happy, and she was certain that without the prince and princess keeping things in turmoil, everyone would be more content. As the northern mountains held bad memories for some of the Skellan, she hoped that the offer of more land would be a further enticement to the other elves.

When Thomaline's grandmother, the former Queen Leonde and her assistants had crafted and established the new Ward, it had been far more flexible than Thomaline had at first realized. Her main concern at the time had been to have permanent viewing posts established so that Goldenfell could still observe what went on in the lands outside of its borders. She did not want to be hampered as they had been in the past, by the lack of knowledge regarding events in those lands. It had been a huge bonus to find out that the borders could be manipulated in some ways. The first improvement was that the Ward had encompassed a larger area than the original boundary of Goldenfell as set by the old Ward. The northern mountains where the Skellan had previously been forced to make their home were now within the new confines of Goldenfell, as was much more of the high plains. Soldiers had been dispatched to thoroughly explore those areas to ensure that no Xarlerii or any other unpleasant surprises had been trapped on the Goldenfell side of the boundary and it had been a relief to all when no threat had been found. For the first year after Thomaline had new outposts established near the observation portals, only in the east and southern areas had these camps become permanently staffed as Men controlled the lands on the other side of the Ward. In the north and northeast, as no inhabitants, Men or otherwise had been observed, the boundaries had slowly been pushed outward for the past year and those camps had remained mobile. As time had passed, many of the soldiers had been asking General Temor if these outposts would also become permanent settlements. This action had almost doubled the size of mountain and plains areas and new herds of wild cattle, horses and other livestock had been gathered into the domain of Goldenfell. It had also allowed more wildlife to mingle with Goldenfell's indigenous flora and fauna for the betterment of all. Thomaline had no worries as to the land's ability to sustain them, even if she were to give up some of that land to the Skellan Elves. She still had plans to move the boundaries a little further, as long as no one else was claiming the area.

"This might split up new families." General Temor cautioned.

"I hope not. I will not force anyone to leave that wishes to stay." Thomaline told her Council, although she was adamant that sentiment would not apply to Prince Cathos. In regard to his sister, that would be decided based on her reaction to Thomaline's proposal. "I would think that some of the Skellan might wish to stay and even some of our own people might move to the proposed new settlement. The newly expanded areas within Goldenfell might also entice more of our own people to expand and create new settlements and I would like to encourage expansion. We have increased the area of Goldenfell by more than half again. We have room for our people to spread out, especially as our Ward is keeping us fully secure. I think that it is time for a little more freedom and choice in setting up accommodations than past circumstances have allowed some of our people."

The Council's many excited voices continued to clamor over one another as they all talked about Thomaline's proposal. All that was, except Skith. He sat quietly, watching the others, but clearly lost in thought and not joining the general discussion.

Thomaline leaned past General Temor to speak with Skith while everyone else was occupied. "What is it Skith? Do you foresee a major problem?"

Skith straightened in his chair before turning to answer. "No. Nothing major. I was just considering what possibilities might play out, but I think it is a good plan. I just am wondering about my own future."

"Would you like to discuss this more privately?" Thomaline asked while the others were still distracted by their own discussions.

"Yes. I think I would. If you have time, may we speak after this council session is over?"

"Of course. When we are finished here." Thomaline agreed although she was slightly shocked by Skith's reactions. While he would often contemplate in silence, she had never seen him so remorseful. It must be the princess that had him so disturbed, she thought.

Both Thomaline and Skith returned to the present Council discussion and soon everyone was involved except Brandt. Sitting to Thomaline's right, he was keeping his silence, however. He had been following most of the conversations, picking up bits and pieces that he would bring to Thomaline's attention later in case she had missed something. He too, was disturbed by his great-grandfather's reticence. He had expected much more input from the Head of the Queen's Council.

When the Council meeting was over and everyone appeared to be on board with the idea of offering the Skellan Elves the proposed alternative to living amongst the Goldenfell Elves, Thomaline formalized her plan to speak with Prince Cathos and Princess Agretha as soon as possible. Firstly, however, she needed to speak privately with Skith. Something was clearly troubling him and she was sure it was the princess. As soon as the others had filed out of the room, Thomaline bade Brandt go and close the Council Room doors.

"Before I reveal my plan to the Skellan, please tell me what is troubling you." she quietly asked Skith.

Before he replied, Skith rose and began to pace before the fireplace. "As you might have guessed, it is Princess Agretha that concerns me. I know that you are keen to have her and her brother out of the fortress and I understand why you feel the way you do, My Lady. The pair have made your life quite uncomfortable for a while now. I suppose that I am just conflicted about her leaving."

"I can certainly understand those feelings, Skith. We have all observed that you and the princess have become remarkably close, but I will not put up with their demands and interference any longer. They do not cease!" Thomaline's voice rose at just the thought of the pair's past grievances.

Skith sighed, "I have tried speaking with Agretha and every time, she promises that she will mend her ways, but then the prince will come along and rile her up again. I believe he does it on purpose! I think that if Agretha were to be left alone, she would be much more amenable."

Thomaline thought there may be some truth in that, but Goldenfell had one ruler, and it was herself. She would not tolerate the princess's constant questioning of her judgement and the sly machinations of the prince any longer. If Agretha and by extension, Skith were to suffer from her plan, it would have to be, even if she were sorry to see Skith hurt.

"If they accept my idea, she will not be exiled Skith. You and the princess will still be able see each other and if you are correct in blaming Prince Cathos for much of the unrest their comments have caused then maybe the situation will improve with time. The princess will still be welcome in Goldenspire if she wishes to visit, but I will not have my hospitality abused by them in the future as they have done since we first offered them sanctuary. After Cathos leaves, I do not want him to even visit!"

"What if I chose to leave? Would you allow that?"

Thomaline was shocked by those questions. "Skith! I would hope you know that you are free to choose as you wish. I admit that I would not want to lose you as my advisor, but I meant what I said to the Council earlier. Skellan Elves may stay and Goldenfell Elves may leave as they wish. The only person I truly want to get permanently out from underfoot is Prince Cathos."

"Do you think that Princess Agretha would leave the resettlement of their people to her brother?" Skith asked as he stopped to stand before Thomaline.

"In truth, no. She is clearly the more able of the two to administer that situation, but that does not mean she must stay away once the move has been made. The pair are at loose ends here in Goldenspire and that has left them with nothing to occupy their time other than shadowing my movements and second guessing my words. They need purpose once more and a resettlement project will achieve that."

Skith gave Thomaline a small smile, "You are probably right. If we can give the prince something to do, other than to plot and complain, most of the battle will be won."

Brandt remained skeptical that the problem prince would be so easily diverted. While the princess did not appear to have ulterior plans, he knew full well that the prince's ultimate goal was to replace Brandt and even eventually try to assume the kingship of Goldenfell.

"I will speak to them both early tomorrow. If that does not go too badly, I will call a larger meeting that will include our Council and more of their people. We will need a better idea of what they think they will need if they are to resettle." Thomaline and Skith continued to work out more details of her plan and the Councilor regained more of his former self-assurance. Brandt knew that things would either work out or not, as much of the responsibility for the success of the Skellan move would be borne by Prince Cathos and his sister.

Brandt believed that Princess Agretha's constant offers of unwanted advice and in some cases criticism of Thomaline's methods and judgements, stemmed from boredom as much as anything. The Skellan Elves had integrated well into Goldenspire society, leaving Agretha less with which to concern herself. While she dealt with minor day-to-day concerns, all decisions of consequence were up to Thomaline as she was the Queen. It must have galled the princess to have handed over that power when they had accepted Thomaline's offer of sanctuary, no matter how much she and her people may have benefitted.

Prince Cathos was another matter. Sly and foolish he might appear, but underneath was a cunning and a resolve to better his station to that which he thought he deserved. Although he and his sister had ruled the Skellan Elves after the death of their former king, Brandt was sure that in matters of consequence, Cathos believed he was the more important of the two. It remained to be seen, which was more important to the prince; Thomaline or her throne, but to Brandt's eyes, the prince was clearly trying to find a way to get both.

The real surprise for Brandt was how Thomaline was treating Skith. She and her Councilor had a stormy history as the two butted heads on a regular basis. To see her talking so kindly with Skith and his apparent lack of confidence was out of character for both. True, it had been Brandt that had caused much of the consternation between the pair and Leonde's revelation of Brandt's true heritage had only lessened the animosity between himself and Skith, not alleviated the matter entirely. To learn that Skith's only son had been Brandt's grandfather had been a shock to all, but at least the fact that he had elven blood explained why he had not noticeably aged since arriving in Goldenfell and the news had somewhat lessened the objections to his position as Consort to the Queen. The relationships amongst himself, Thomaline and Skith were still undergoing changes, however.

Brandt's musings and Thomaline and Skith's conversation were interrupted by a knock on the Council door. Brandt went to answer as their time in the Council Chambers was rarely disturbed.

"What is it? What is wrong?" he asked the messenger who waited with the guards.

"There's been another message, My Lord. It's that River Lord again. He is still asking for a meeting."

CHAPTER THREE

Thomaline's temper had returned, and Brandt was glad that she had asked Skith to accompany them to the meeting with the prince and princess. He still did not understand why some things upset her so easily lately, but Brandt would back up Thomaline's actions no matter what. He hoped that Skith's presence would give the meeting a more civil tone. The fact that Prince Cathos was late to the meeting did nothing to lessen Thomaline's temper and all Brandt could do was reach for her hand and hold it reassuringly, out of sight and under the table. Although she did not look at Brandt as the prince finally sauntered into the room, the squeeze of her hand let him know that she appreciated the gesture.

"I am sorry Thomaline, your servant has only just found me. I gather that you wanted to speak with Agretha and myself?" The prince stated as he looked around before choosing a seat. Thomaline did not need Sullan's presence to know that what she had just heard was a lie. Cathos had been informed of their meeting over an hour ago! Thomaline merely tipped her head in acknowledgement and smiled coolly as she watched the prince finally seat himself beside his sister at the other end of the table.

"Why did you summon us?" Agretha wanted to know. Her words were for Thomaline, but she looked directly at Skith as she asked. Both royals ignored Brandt.

"After much deliberation, I have decided upon a proposal that I wish to share with you." Thomaline began. "You have both been more than forthcoming with your thoughts about how I should rule here in Goldenspire, especially concerning your people and I have given your ideas due consideration." Agretha and Cathos both brightened at her words and Cathos's eyes gleamed in anticipation. "I have decided that everyone concerned might be happier if a new settlement were to be built."

"A new settlement? Where? For whom?" This had not been what Princess Agretha had expected, but she at least appeared intrigued.

"I do not understand how a new settlement would make anyone happier." Prince Cathos stated, the earlier gleam gone from his eyes and replaced by suspicion and anger.

"You have both on many occasions voiced your concerns and I think that establishing a new settlement for the Skellan Elves, either in the mountains or the plains surrounding the area where you formerly lived, will solve many problems." Thomaline paused briefly but went on before either of the twins could comment or object. "Goldenfell will of course supply all the necessary materials, supplies, livestock, equipment and what have you, to help you establish your own community. That area of Goldenfell will be yours and it will be up to you to pick the spot or spots for settlement. You will once again be in charge and responsible for the lives of your people."

"When will you have us leave?" Agretha asked warily. The idea appealed but of course there were reservations.

"I think that you should speak with your people and decide that for yourself." Thomaline said. "It will soon be summer, and I would think that you would like to have your new homes built before winter sets in. In that regard, I would suggest sooner than later. If you and Prince Cathos speak with your people today, tomorrow my Council and I would like to go over some of the details of the move with you and your representatives. Once we know what you will require, I do not think that it will take too long to organize." She said with confidence.

Now it was Princess Agretha's eyes that gleamed. She was already making mental plans before being interrupted by her brother.

"You wish to exile us back to that miserable place in the mountains? You are going back on your word and your invitation to have us live here!" Cathos was not happy at this turn of events. His pursuit of Thomaline would be greatly hampered from such a distance as would other things.

"On the contrary. I am going back on nothing. You have constantly stated your unhappiness with your accommodation and conditions of living within my Goldenspire. I am simply trying to correct that problem. I thought you would be glad to get out from under my thumb, so to speak. I will leave the details to you and your sister, but I am not exiling anyone. Those that wish to stay here may do so, as well as any from Goldenfell who wish, may leave, and resettle in the lands I will set aside for you." Cathos thought he had found a loophole in that statement, but before he could speak, Thomaline continued, "I know that you and Agretha would not abandon your people and so of course you will lead and be responsible for them in your new home."

Princess Agretha looked as if she would like to keep her brother quiet and jumped back into the conversation before he could reply to Thomaline.

"Of course, we will accept your offer. I for one, cannot wait to tell our people. I am sure that most will accept. We will speak with them and be happy to meet with you tomorrow."

Thomaline and Brandt could see that the princess was genuine in her excitement and even Skith looked heartened by her enthusiasm. It was only Prince Cathos that was unhappy with the proposal.

"Very well. I am revising my thoughts as I now imagine that there will be many that wish to attend our meeting tomorrow. Why do we not have it in the courtyard and open the meeting up to all the people, yours as well as mine, that wish to attend." Thomaline hoped that greater attendance would help to quell any negativity her decision might raise.

Soon, initial plans were made, and the prince found himself being drawn from the room by his extremely excited sister. Thomaline asked Skith to speak with the rest of the Council so that they could inform every one of the upcoming meeting and would then be ready for the open meeting the next day. When Skith had left, Thomaline turned to Brandt, "That went much better than I had expected."

"Yes, she surprised me. Agretha was so enthused by the idea that she didn't give Cathos much chance to object. He's probably still wondering how his plans went astray." Brandt laughed. He was glad to see that Thomaline's anger had dissipated and that she had brightened up as much as the princess.

"No doubt he will try to spoil things, but I will leave him to his sister for now. She can deal with him. I want to go for a ride. I want to get out of this fortress for a while."

"Where will we go?" Brandt was game to leave as well. Lately he had taken to spending much more of his time inside Goldenspire to stay closer to

Thomaline. He had run interference between her and the Skellan royals for quite some time now and he was as weary of the situation as Thomaline, but he at least had a few diversions of his own. Brandt had continued training sessions with Arms Master Greth and had begun to explore the art of making weapons and armor to divert him from palace concerns. Thomaline rarely had the luxury to pursue arts merely for pleasure although she still managed some training with Greth.

"We will ride into the mountains. I want to see Leonde."

Thomaline's grandmother, the former Queen Leonde, lived in the mountains over an hour's ride north from Goldenspire. She had lived there in her modest cottage since leaving the kingdom to her son, Leyrd, but after Leonde returned to her home following the battle with the Xarlerii, Thomaline had insisted that Leonde take a few more comforts with her. To that end, two new cottages had been built near Leonde's home to house the two servants and the two guards that had been sent to see to the needs of the elderly elf.

"I'll send word to the stables." Brandt offered.

"Yes, do that. I need to find Skith and inform him of our departure and I want to take a few things with us to Leonde. I will meet you in the courtyard within half an hour." Thomaline smiled happily at Brandt and left the room in search of her Councilor. Brandt followed her out the door, but their routes diverged as he turned towards their apartment. He wanted to change before riding out.

Soon, Brandt was at the stables, dressed more appropriately for riding while still being armed and he watched as the grooms led the horses out. These were two new mounts, and both were fractious as they had not been ridden for a few days. The horses were brothers and were bred to run. Thomaline's was a tall black horse while Brandt's was a blood-bay, and both horses were stallions.

"They are very eager, My Lord." Said one of the grooms as he fought to control Thomaline's horse.

"I can see that."

"See what?" Thomaline asked as she joined Brandt. She too had changed and somewhere in her travels she had found Alred. The cat looked eager to join them for their trip.

"We can see that the horses are eager to be going for a run." Brandt told her.

"I know. I am sorry Arden." she said to her mount as she took the reins from the groom and quietly went about settling the horse. "I should have been here sooner. You must be getting very bored." She told the horse. The animal snorted and shook his head, sending his long mane rippling along his neck and then he started to impatiently paw the ground as Thomaline secured the saddlebag she had been carrying to the back of her saddle. When she was through, she quickly sprang up into the saddle before Arden could do anything to object. This horse was vastly different in temperament from her last mount. Arden was more headstrong than most and it had taken Thomaline's unique rapport with animals to finally break through the barrier that had kept the elven trainers from taming the animal. Although tame was not a word Brandt would have used to describe the horse. He did not know what exactly Thomaline had been able to show the horse to get his co-operation, but they had finally seemed to reach a truce of sorts. Brandt jumped onto the saddle of his much quieter mount as well and the pair were soon thundering out the front gate, racing towards the mountain trail that led to Leonde's cottage while Alred kept pace beside them.

Ten minutes later, Thomaline and Brandt were quietly walking their mounts along the trail. With their first burst of energy worn off, the animals were content to keep to the slower pace. For now. Alred had run ahead and soon disappeared, and Brandt doubted they would see him again until they reached Leonde's.

"What did you bring?" he asked.

"I picked up a few things from the kitchens. I know that fruit cake is a favorite of Leonde's and Cook made some yesterday."

"That doesn't look like it's all fruit cake." He said, indicating the bulging saddlebag.

"Just a few things that she left in Goldenspire. I thought she would like to have them back."

"Hmm. What did Skith say when you told him we were leaving?"

"He did not question our visit to Leonde. He was preoccupied with the details for tomorrow's meeting, and he was with Agretha. At least they were both smiling when I saw them." It had been good to see. There had been too few smiles between the pair lately.

As they rode along, Brandt's horse suddenly started and began to sidle as he tried to turn back the way they had come. Something to their rear had caught his attention and now Thomaline's horse began to rear in response.

"What is it? What do you see?" Thomaline asked as she brought her horse under control. She could hear a disturbance in the brush, further back and hidden by a bend in the trail.

"I can't see anything! Let's keep moving!" Brandt said and Thomaline agreed by putting her heels to her horse. It could have been anything from a bear to a wild cat. Yaral were not the only mountain cats, although normally most of the larger animals, predators or prey did not wander this close to Goldenspire. Whatever it was, Brandt did not want to tackle the problem with just their swords and his and Thomaline's hunting bows. As their horses jumped into another run, Thomaline and Brandt missed seeing the cause of the commotion behind them.

They were out of sight by the time a limping figure crashed through the underbrush, onto the road. Prince Cathos swore as he dusted himself off and straightened his torn jacket. It would be a long walk back to the fortress if he could not catch his horse. He still did not know what had set the stupid animal off, but it would be sorry when he found it! Now he would not be able to discover what Thomaline and the Man were up to. The prince should have been paying more attention to his surroundings. If he had, he might have seen the cause of his debacle, crouched in the brush, just off the road.

Previously, Alred had been prowling through the forest as Thomaline and Brandt walked their horses along the path, until he had been attracted by a stealthy noise not too far away. Intrigued, he had paused to circle back and investigate. He was not consciously trying to protect his elven partners as much as he was simply curious and when he had found a horse and rider hiding in the bushes, Alred had seen an opportunity. The fact that it was Prince Cathos made his actions all the more appealing. He jumped out from the underbrush near the rear of the duo, startling the horse and causing it to buck and pitch its rider. Alred had then chased the unfortunate gelding until it had been in a full and terrified flight. The rider would never catch it now. Upon his return from the chase, Alred retreated once more into the bushes when he saw the fallen rider regain his feet. Alred did not like the Skellan and especially not the prince.

None of the yaral wanted any contact with them and to an animal, they avoided Cathos.

When the Skellan had first come to Goldenspire and while Thomaline had been recovering from her injuries received in the battle with the Xarlerii, the prince had tried to win over Alred's affection, but the cat had not so gently rebuffed the advances. When this had happened, the prince's anger had been directed at all the yaral that crossed his path and one day he had struck out with his quirt and then kicked and one of the young new yaral that had not moved out of the way of the prince's anger. Alred had seen and since that day, he had found ways to take a cat's revenge. With the prince's scent easy to find, his possessions had steadily been "misplaced," or they vanished entirely. One of Alred's better chances happened when the unwary prince stood with his back to the cat while the prince was waiting for an audience with Thomaline. While no one noticed, Alred had casually stretched out a claw and hooked a thread that dangled from the seam of the prince's trouser seat, causing a large split to appear. When the prince stood before Thomaline and bowed, all those who were standing behind had enjoyed the show and the prince's humiliation! Only Thomaline had looked thoughtfully at her pet when Alred had come to take his place beside her chair. Alred's pastime was still going strong while the prince seemed none the wiser.

This last 'game' had been a brief, but exciting encounter for Alred and once the prince was on the road, limping back to Goldenspire, Alred turned away to resume his run up the mountain. Usually, Thomaline's presence served to curb the cat's more playful tendencies and so this unexpected opportunity had been rousing!

Soon the horses had run out their nervousness and once again Thomaline and Brandt settled them into a steady walk and even when Alred crashed out of the trees and onto the trail, the animals barely batted an eye towards the disturbance. Nonetheless, Brandt was happy when Leonde's little clearing came into view. As if she had been expecting them, Leonde stood on the front steps, waiting for them.

"Good day. I am pleased that you have come to see me." Leonde greeted them.

"Good day to you as well, Leonde. Unfortunately, matters have kept me far too busy recently, but today I am taking a little time for myself." Thomaline told her grandmother.

"Will you stay for a meal?"

"We'd be pleased to join you." Brandt answered for them as he dismounted. When Thomaline had done the same, he took her horse's reins and led both mounts towards the small stable. There, he was joined by the two guards that lived with Leonde. The three were soon in a discussion.

"You are looking especially radiant today." Leonde complemented Thomaline as they walked towards the cottage door.

"Thank you." she laughed. "I am sure that is due to being free of Goldenspire for a while."

"Is it Goldenspire or something else?"

"It is happiness. I had my talk with Agretha and Cathos today and outlined my plan to have them move back to where we found them. We are having a general meeting tomorrow for anyone who wishes to join us, and I will outline the plan for all." Thomaline had discussed the bare bones of her idea the last time she and her grandmother had met.

"I am curious. What was the reaction of the prince and princess?" Leonde asked as she motioned for Thomaline to sit at the table. It was larger than the previous one that had sat near the cottage door and there were now five chairs and a bench against the wall. Leonde shared her meals with the two elves assigned to see to her needs and her two guardsmen.

"He is NOT pleased, but he could hardly say anything negative when his sister was all but bouncing on her chair with excitement. She is very eager for the move and was already making plans with Skith as they left the Council Chambers."

"Yes, she has a purpose once more. I always believed she would be receptive to the idea of setting up their own hold again."

"She never even entertained the idea that Cathos might not want to go with her, she just started making plans. I do not think that he will be able to find an excuse to stay behind that she would accept."

"Even if he does find one, I'll make sure that he goes." Brandt stated as he entered the cottage and handed Thomaline her saddle bag. "I don't care if no one else choses to leave, but he will not remain!"

"That is very good to hear." Leonde smiled at Brandt before asking Thomaline, "What have you brought me today?"

"Cook had made fruit cakes, and I managed to liberate two for you." Thomaline replied and took the bag from Brandt's hand so that she could delve inside for the cakes.

"That's not all you brought. I thought you said the rest was some of Leonde's things." Brandt said as he watched Thomaline pass the cakes to Leonde.

"Trust your curiosity to make you snoop. I brought something that Leonde wished to see." Thomaline reached once more into the bag and brought out two items. The first was a small parcel of Leonde's possessions, but the other was something quite different. "I have brought the messages. The last one just arrived." The messages were the missives that had been received over the past two years from someone purporting to be 'The River Lord.' There were eight in all.

Leonde reached for the items and Brandt could have sworn that he heard her quietly mutter a few very bad words. The act of swearing seemed to be catching.

CHAPTER FOUR

"I do not understand how these messages are getting through to us." Thomaline complained. "I thought the Ward would keep out everything with the exception being the weather."

"It should. I too, want to understand how this is happening. That is why I asked to see the messages themselves." Leonde spread the notes on the table in front of her. There should not be a way for these parchments to pass the barrier of the Ward! True, the weather could not be kept out, but nothing physical should be able to get through. "I would like to keep these for a while. It may take some time to learn all that I can. Have you responded to any?"

"No! That would only give them proof that we are here, and I will not risk opening the Ward." Only Thomaline and Leonde had the power to open any of the observation portals.

"I am afraid that someone already has and knows we are here." Leonde stated. There was no guesswork in the messages. Whoever had sent the missives knew that Thomaline was Queen even if they had not mentioned her by name.

The first message had been found just weeks after the new Ward had been established. One of the guards at the new outpost in the south had discovered the note lying near the Ward boundary. That one had been followed by a new message every season; all were addressed to the Queen of Goldenfell with regards from the River Lord. He kept requesting an audience.

"It must be from one of the forts by the river. This 'River Lord' is probably their leader." Brandt reasoned.

"I agree, but how do they know about me? How do they know that there is a Queen and not a King? The old Ward was only taken down for a few days before the new one was put in place. There was not enough time for anyone to come from the river and learn what was transpiring in Goldenfell and we did not find anyone that was trapped here after the new Ward was installed. No one should even guess that we are here. After all, it has been eighty years since we initially closed off this land from the world of Men. They did not know of our existence then and even if they did, there would be none left that would have remembered us, even if they had known exactly where we were." Thomaline lamented.

"No one would have had time to reach us from outside, but what about someone from here, leaving to go to the river?" This was the only explanation that Brandt could see as a possibility. Someone had to have betrayed their presence to this 'River Lord'.

"You mean Mendeth do you not?" Leonde asked. The name had not been forgotten.

"Yes. We never found him after he escaped from Goldenspire. He would have had ample time to get to the border before the new Ward would have stopped him." Brandt agreed. "He could have heard all about your plans for the new Ward before he escaped. Who knows what else he might have learned after his cell was found to be empty."

General Temor had interrogated all the soldiers who had been responsible for guarding the former councilor, but no clues had been discovered as to how he had escaped or to where he had gone. After Mendeth had disappeared and had never been seen again, the search had eventually been discontinued.

"Maybe, but I cannot discern why he would give the knowledge of Goldenfell's existence to any Man. What would he have to gain?" This was a discussion that Brandt and Thomaline had entertained more than once, and she still had come to no certainty as to an answer. Surely Mendeth's hatred of Brandt would not have led him to betray all of Goldenfell, especially to more Men. If he was now outside of the kingdom, how had he gotten the messages through?

"No matter for the moment," Leonde said, "I will return to Goldenspire within the next few days and by then, maybe I can shed more light on the problem. If not, I will confer with the others who helped in making the Ward. For now, let us speak of other things. Tell me, what else has been happening since I have been gone?"

Thomaline frowned but bent to Leonde's wish and the conversation turned to more mundane talk with a little gossip thrown in until a brief time later, a loud yowl was heard at the cottage door. Alred had arrived and wanted in to join them.

"I see he has finally learned a few manners." said Leonde as she rose to open her door. When she did, the cat walked in and moved to sit beside Thomaline.

"Only with you." Thomaline ruefully admitted as she placed her hand on Alred's head. Leonde just smiled and closed her door. Alred might be Thomaline's pet, but he was still very independent. With Leonde, however, he obeyed because she would have it no other way.

"Brandt, please call the others. I believe that our meal is ready." Leonde said as she moved towards the hearth.

Soon, the guards and retainers joined them, and large platters of food were set before them all. Brandt had never asked, but he was certain that among Leonde's many gifts, the power of precognition was present. From the size of the meal, it was as if Leonde had known they were coming. It was the best time that Thomaline and Brandt had had spent in a long while.

Much later, as they rode through the dark on the trail back towards Goldenspire, Brandt asked, "Do you think she will be able to learn how those messages keep getting through the barrier?"

"I hope she can learn how this is happening. With the continual arrival of these messages, I am afraid that our Ward might once again be under attack. That or there is a defect that we have not yet discovered." Thomaline reasoned. Why else were the messages appearing? Did the River Lord pose a threat or were his messages to warn Goldenfell?

"Leonde has not sensed any interference and there have been no reports from the guard posts of anything suspicious happening on the other side of the ward. I should think that we would know by now if there was someone attacking the shield." At least Brandt hoped that they would know.

Thomaline sighed. "I know Leonde has not been able to discern anything, but how else could those messages be appearing. It is like magic."

Magic. Could that be the answer? "Maybe it is." Said Brandt. "Think about it from that point of view. Could someone be using their own magic to make those messages appear? Maybe the source is not from beyond, but from our side of the Ward. Maybe there is no River Lord, only someone set upon causing mayhem."

Thomaline stopped her horse to peer at Brandt through the gloom of the night and then she smiled. "You might just be on to the answer!" With that, Thomaline dug her heels into Arden's sides, and they wasted no time on the rest of the return journey to Goldenspire. Thomaline needed to speak with Skith.

As soon as they entered the courtyard, Brandt and Thomaline threw their reins to the waiting grooms and Thomaline shouted for one of the guards to take word to Lord Skith and General Temor that she needed to speak with them. Urgently! Brandt jogged along beside her as she ran up the stairs of the fortress. Within moments, Skith joined them and Thomaline led them towards the Council Chambers where the General soon arrived.

"What is it, My Queen?" asked Temor once they were all inside the Chamber and the doors were shut and guarded.

"We have been to see Leonde, and I have given her the River Lord messages to investigate, but on the way back Brandt said something that I agree might be the answer as to what we may have overlooked."

"What is that?" Skith asked.

"What if the messages are not coming from the other side of the Ward at all? What if they are being created here, by someone who is already in Goldenfell?"

Both Skith and Temor looked at each as they thought about what Thomaline had said. They had not thought of that complication.

"Who do you think is responsible?" Skith asked.

"It is more than just the messages." Thomaline stated. "It is the timing of them as well. We have discussed this with Leonde and there was only one name that fits the situation." She said as she looked to Skith for his reaction.

"Mendeth?" Temor asked.

"Mendeth." Brandt confirmed. "The timeline was too tight for anyone but him to have been involved. He escaped and then disappeared entirely. It's been two years, and no trace has ever been found of him. He could be here or on the other side of the Ward. Also, for the River Lord, if he exists, to know that there was a Queen, someone from Goldenfell must have told him. Men don't even know that Goldenfell exists!"

"How do you think Mendeth is involved with the messages?" Skith wanted to know.

Thomaline ignored the question for the moment and asked instead, "Who was Mendeth close to? Did he have any friends or family that thought as he did regarding Brandt?" Mendeth had plotted Brandt's removal for years before the elf had been dismissed from the Council. He must surely have had other associates that thought as he did.

"Besides myself? Is that what you are asking?" Skith began to draw himself up in haughtiness.

"No! That is not what she is asking. This is not about you, Skith!" Brandt angrily braced Skith. Mendeth was still a very touchy subject between the councilor and Brandt.

Thomaline hurried on before the two could engage in further argument. "We have overlooked the fact that Mendeth must have had other friends or conspirators. I did not think that it would have been possible for him to escape from Goldenspire, but he did. I think now that he must have had help in that regard even though we could not find anyone during our first investigation. I also think that it is possible for him to still be in contact with this person or persons, in some way. Skith, you knew him the best. Who would be the most likely to help Mendeth?"

Skith frowned, but answered, "I do not know My Lady. I will have to think on the matter, but Mendeth never said much about his past or family and we did not spend time discussing our lives. He was very loyal to your uncle and always wanted what was best for the kingdom. If he had an accomplice, I do not know who it might be."

"Let me ask a few questions around the fortress." General Temor said. "Give me a day or two and I might be able to supply a name."

Brandt thought that of the two, Temor stood a much better chance of discovering information than Skith. The General was very well liked, and he would know where to ask such questions.

"Yes. Please do so Temor. The more I think about it, the more I am convinced that someone from within Goldenfell is helping this River Lord through Mendeth. Remember, Mendeth was able to use one of the talismans that was created to breach a gap in the old Ward. He should never have been able to do such a thing, but he managed somehow. That bespeaks a strong power or magic that we did not know he possessed, and he might be using that ability or some other we do not know about, to link with someone here."

"It must be someone here in Goldenspire." Said Temor. "I will find who among our people is a traitor.

"No." said Brandt as he thought more on Mendeth's previous actions. "Do not limit your search to just the Goldenfell Elves. If Skith cannot think of anyone that would help Mendeth, then it makes sense that it could be one of the Skellan. Mendeth escaped just after they arrived here and remember, he was with them in the mountains long enough to have made a new friend or two." Prince Cathos came to mind.

"The Skellan do not possess any magic. How would they be able to create these messages here, in Goldenfell?" asked Skith.

"They told us that they do not have any active magic, but who knows what abilities may lie dormant. I think Brandt is correct. Skith, concentrate your inquiries among the Skellan. Temor, I want you to collaborate with Lord Skith, but I wish for you to concern yourself with our people, especially anyone in the border settlements. Someone must be assisting with these communications, and I want to know who is responsible. Right now, that is more important than worrying about what this River Lord wants." stated Thomaline. "We still need to be ready for tomorrow's meeting about the Skellan re-settlement." When the others had left, she and Brandt were soon on their way to their own rooms where Alred was already waiting.

"I thought we were done with Mendeth." Brandt lamented as he started to undress.

"It now appears that is unlikely, but we will get to the bottom of these messages, and I will put a stop to them."

Brandt hoped that Thomaline would be proven correct. Maybe if the Skellan all left, the problem would go away as well. It was a nice thought, but he did not put much stock in the theory. This particular problem would never be solved so easily.

"Regardless of how they are appearing, will you find out what this River Lord wants?" Brandt asked Thomaline as she emerged from the bathing room.

"I have given it thought, but I have not decided. On one hand, I do not wish to give confirmation to the notion that Goldenfell and her Elves really do exist, but I must admit that I am very curious about this person. I suppose that learning what he wants might be prudent." Thomaline answered as she crawled into their bed. "I will keep thinking upon it." Regardless of what she had said earlier, she did believe that there was a River Lord but whether or not Mendeth was with him was another question.

Brandt left to take his turn preparing for bed and Alred seized the opportunity to help himself to Brandt's side of the bed. By the time Brandt returned, Thomaline was asleep, and the huge cat was lying beside her. After having only limited success in shoving the cat over to try and make more room for himself, Brandt climbed into bed and the small space that was left to him. It was only the fact that Thomaline was already asleep that left the struggle between cat and Man for another time. It had been a long and tiring day for Thomaline and Brandt did not want to disturb her rest by causing Alred to vocalize his displeasure at being disturbed. He would let Alred keep his place, for now. As he lay waiting for sleep to overtake him, Brandt thought about Mendeth. While he had been a councilor, Mendeth had wanted to rid Goldenfell of Brandt through whatever means necessary, and Brandt doubted that Mendeth's goal had changed. He might even be more determined. How he had gotten the River Lord involved was just as big a mystery. Why would this person want to speak with Thomaline? And how would that benefit Mendeth? As Brandt began to finally drift off, one last thought occurred. Had Mendeth once again found a replacement for the position of Consort?

EVERY DAY WAS TORTURE. Home no longer called, but in his heart, he could still feel its tug. Soon he would have to try to find his way there no matter what messages were received!

CHAPTER FIVE

Brandt flinched as the outer door to their rooms burst open and then shut with a large bang. Evidently, Thomaline was once again upset. He sighed as he thought about Thomaline's mood swings and tempers. He had not seen this much volatility and drama since his younger sister had entered her teens! He turned around, but Thomaline was already entering the bathing room and the door to that room was slammed as well. He guessed this current mood had been brought on when the continuing discussions for the Skellan resettlement had not progressed as well as Thomaline would have liked. Brandt did not know this for certain as he had left the day's talks after a brief time, seeing that his input was in no way heeded or even wanted in the many discussions the day had produced. Moving the Skellan was going to be a bigger problem than they had anticipated.

To escape the endless politics and not so polite rhetoric, Brandt had gone to the yaral barracks and spent a quite hour or two with Tallee, the elf in charge of the yaral. There, they had discussed the ongoing training for the soldier and yaral pairs of the Queen's Brigade and mused over all the yaral's continued disdain of the Skellan elves. After a couple of pints of ale that Tallee fetched from his room he finally shared his opinion about what was causing the yaral's attitude of scorn towards the Skellan soldiers that had wanted to join the paired unit. Now, if Thomaline would calm down a little, he would share what he had learned.

It was a while later, but Thomaline finally emerged from her solitude and began poking through her wardrobe looking for something to wear for the upcoming evening meal.

"The banquet is still on?" Brandt ventured as he watched her select a colorful and ornate tunic with matching trousers to wear for the meal. Unlike the princess, Thomaline never wore a dress, but the emerald green of the garments as well as the ornate gold stitching, perfectly set off Thomaline's beauty and golden hair. She claimed a dress would never work with her sword and dagger.

"Yes." She seemed quite calm now. "There will be about forty or so in attendance and we will try and finalize the plans for the relocation."

"So, you did make progress?"

"Of course. Why would you think that we did not?" Thomaline was surprised that Brandt did not know what had been achieved throughout the day.

"Well, I wasn't there for the last bit or even the bit before that. I left and was following up on something else."

Thomaline had not realized that Brandt had left the courtyard so early. Now that she thought about the matter, she realized that he had been uncommonly quite after the first hour or two.

"Where did you go?"

"I'll tell you all about it later. Right now, I'd like to hear what happened in your meetings."

Thomaline quickly finished dressing and sat on the bed before explaining what had been agreed to with the Skellan and all other interested parties. Princess Agretha had already been remarkably busy before the meeting, talking with many of her people and promoting a move to new settlements. Most had eventually become enthusiastic about the plan and had needed little more persuasion once they realized that the move would be fully supported and supplied by Thomaline and Goldenspire's supplies. The only real dissention had come from some of Prince Cathos's followers. As per his usual tactic, the prince himself said little against the move and had left it up to his lackeys to try and spoil the plan. Thankfully, Princess Agretha had a lifetime's experience in dealing with her twin and the dissenters' objections were quickly and firmly explained away or discredited. Unfortunately, this had still wasted valuable time and as a result there were a few items to be resolved.

"They are really going to leave?" Brandt was amazed that plans had come together so well in the few hours after he had slipped away. Maybe he should have stayed.

"Oh yes. Tonight, we will hopefully see to the last details and tomorrow there will be another meeting with people who are having difficulty deciding if they should stay or go. I want to make sure that it is known that there is no right or wrong decision. People are not being forced into choosing a one-way move. I expect many will want to move back and forth as their situations deem fit. The only one that will not have that option is Cathos. Him, I do not want to ever see here again!" Thomaline still had not found a way to keep the prince from returning to Goldenspire but with Brandt's help, she hoped to have a clearer idea in the next few days.

As Brandt moved to change his own clothing, he asked Thomaline to fill him in on what he had missed by leaving and as Thomaline obliged, he forgot all about what he had been planning to tell her of his conversation with Tallee.

Later, as the meal wore on, Brandt once again was feeling left out as he listened to Thomaline and Agretha continue to flesh out their plans. As the two leaders sat together, Brandt beside Thomaline with Skith sitting beside Agretha, Brandt's attention began to wander as he heard the ideas and plans discussed. The three of them seemed to have matters well in hand, but he was getting a bit bored. How Thomaline could deal with issues like this on a daily basis was beyond him. He knew well that his attention span and patience would never rise to the level needed for such diplomacy. As he began to entertain himself with watching others at the banquet, he suddenly took notice of the expressions that flitted across the face of Cathos as the prince watched the three making their arrangements. The prince had been seated further down the table and had little inclusion in the plans being made. The fact that he had chosen that seat had proven that he had scant interest in furthering plans for the upcoming move, but the looks being directed towards Thomaline indicated otherwise. He did not like what was happening. Not even a bit!

Brandt continued to observe the prince without Cathos realizing that he was under his scrutiny. The Skellan was planning something. Brandt was sure of it. All his scheming revolved around Thomaline and by extension, the removal of Brandt.

The food had all been cleared away and the last of the supper wine had been drunk by the time the two leaders called a halt to their discussion. Over the last few days, nearly all the immediate details had been finalized and everyone would meet again the next morning, before they all once again met with the people who were undecided about the upcoming separation of the two groups of Elves. No wonder Thomaline was so tired and moody lately. All she did was attend meetings! If they ever got the Skellan off to their own settlements, Brandt was determined to get Thomaline to take more time for herself and put a limit on the number of meetings she had to attend. These days, other than Brandt himself, her main diversion and stress release was the time she spent in training with Arms Master Greth as she had vowed she would be able to keep up with Brandt in skill at arms. Brandt was thankful that she only wanted to be equal and not better as Greth was extremely hard to please, even if she was the Queen.

The group might have stayed in their chairs even longer, but at that moment, Alred made himself known to the lingering diners. The cat had entered the hall earlier but had not stopped to settle by Thomaline as usual. Instead, he had made several forays around the room and had just now returned to studying the prince, unnoticed by most except for Brandt and possibly Thomaline. Alred had sat quietly near the hearth for a while earlier, watching the banquet participants but now he appeared to be giving into his instincts for mischief. As he prowled silently across the floor, he moved directly behind Prince Cathos's chair and then emitted an ear-splitting yowl that had the prince and most of the elves on that side of the table nearly falling from their chairs in shock and fear.

As the prince sprang up angrily to confront Alred, the elf's hand was moving for the sword that he was not wearing. From their position at the head of the table, Brandt and Thomaline could not see the expression on the prince's face, but they all saw his actions. When Prince Cathos remembered he was not wearing a sword, he continued his move until he was grasping the handle of his dagger.

"Cathos! Sit down. It is only Alred." Princess Agretha called loudly to her brother. She had seen his hand on his dagger as had the others and she had moved to allay the situation before it got out of hand. "He is not going to hurt you. He is only playing."

That was a bit of a stretch Brandt thought as he revised his opinion as to the cat's motive. Alred was not up to mischief, and he clearly was not playing with Cathos. Brandt could also see that Alred was in no way intimidated by a dagger and in fact, the cat seemed almost eager for the prince to try his chance. Anyone who knew cats could see by Alred's body language that he was not about to back down. The lashing of his tail showed that he was angry.

Cathos gave the barest of forced laughs as he slowly moved his hand away from his weapon. Someday he would have his reckoning with the problem feline. He would make sure of that.

"Alred! Come here!" Thomaline called sharply to her pet. She knew very well what the animal was doing. She just did not know why.

Alred continued his unblinking stare at Cathos, but finally bent to Thomaline's demand. Just not before giving the Skellan prince a slight curl of his lip and a low growl as he flipped his tail up and casually walked towards Thomaline. The promise of more to come between the two had shone from his eyes. Alred had seen the hatred in the prince's eyes, even if the others could not.

Brandt could only speculate as to what that display had been about. Thomaline too, had to wonder. She made a note to ask around to see if anyone could tell her what Prince Cathos had been up to. It had to be something, because Alred had certainly not been in a playful mood. She was sure that if Cathos had truly pulled his dagger from its sheath, it would have been the last move he ever made.

Agretha too wondered. She knew that Cathos hated the animal, but she could not countenance that he would be careless enough to be drawn into trying to hurt it, especially in front of Thomaline and all these witnesses. How could he hope to make amends to Thomaline for that?

As Thomaline and Brandt returned to their chambers, Alred followed, all the while making small grumbling noises. When they reached their doors, Thomaline had a quiet word with one of the guards before joining Brandt. Alred declined her invitation to enter the royal chambers and instead sat with the remaining guard, watching as the other strode down the corridor and out of sight.

"What was that about?" Brandt asked after Thomaline had closed their doors.

"I asked Bendor to seek information on the doings of Prince Cathos for the past few days. I suspect that he has done something that had attracted Alred's attention. I would like to know what it might have been."

"Then I suspect it must be something serious because Alred certainly was. At first, I thought he was just amusing himself, but that was a direct challenge to Cathos that he made."

"Oh yes! It was definitely that. I will try and find time to see Tallee. Maybe he can help me understand what has riled Alred." Riled may not be the correct word, she thought, murderous might be a better description.

"That reminds me. I was going to tell you earlier, but we got so caught up with the Skellan plans that I forgot. I had quite a long talk with Tallee this afternoon and he thinks he finally understands why the yaral won't have anything to do with the Skellan."

"Well, do not make me guess. What have you learned?"

"It has to do with magic."

"Why would that be? The Skellan do not possess magic."

"That's the point. The yaral won't work with the Skellan because they have no magic. In some way, magic is what binds the elf and yaral partners into a friendship and working relationship. If they cannot bond with someone, they will certainly not be their pet. They aren't ever domestic and only Alred and your previous cats have had any kind of manners. It must be your own abilities that have drawn the yaral to you over the years. We have called them pets but maybe they were more than that."

"You could be correct, but I do not know if I would call it manners, exactly. Alred and the other were just a little better behaved."

"That is due to your influence and the fact that you bring the cats here when they are still kittens, not mostly grown as the other yaral are when they come here. When you were otherwise occupied, you know that there was chaos in the fortress. They only listened to you."

"Hah! You are wrong in that. Alred minds Leonde more than me."

"Everyone minds Leonde! No one, elf or animal would dare to do otherwise." Brandt laughed and Thomaline joined him. He was certainly correct in that. Her grandmother was such a commanding force, the mere thought of going against her wishes was unthinkable. She could be terrifying if challenged.

"I wonder why it has taken Tallee so long to discover this? Has he told anyone else?"

"No. At least I don't think he has. It's only just occurred to him. He says that the cats had an extremely challenging time trying to relay this concept to him. He thinks that it took them quite a long time to figure out the problem themselves. He said that they don't conceive of it as magic the way we might. There was just something missing in the Skellan, and it took time to understand and then an enormous effort on their part to convey that concept to Tallee."

"I really must find the time to speak with him. Maybe as soon as we get this Skellan relocation sorted. Until I do, would you please see him and ask that he not share this knowledge with anyone else? I will need to think on this before trying to explain it to the Skellan. Some of their soldiers will be very disappointed."

"I'll see to it first thing tomorrow, before I go for my ride with Palin. What time are you meeting with the undecided group?"

"Not until after the noon meal. I have a few other things to deal with before then."

"Are you meeting with the Council?"

"No. Not tomorrow morning. Skith thinks he will have things well in hand. He has formed some committees and placed certain Councilors in charge of different projects and Agretha has selected from among her people, representatives to join in, so both our people and the Skellan will have input into all decisions regarding how best to organize the project."

"What about Prince Cathos? What is his role in all of this? Besides stirring up problems that is." Brandt had not seen the prince earlier and doubted that any plans Cathos had would be for leaving Goldenspire.

"I do not know. I am leaving that to Agretha to manage. She has proven in the past that she can effectively deal with her brother. If not, I have a plan or two of my own." Thomaline said with grim determination.

"Yes, well you're not the only one." Brandt thought his plan might be more permanent than Thomaline's.

"Enough of that. I am tired. I have spent the entire day dealing with the Skellan and I would like to relax."

"Would you like me to draw you a bath?" Brandt laughed.

Thomaline laughed in return before giving Brandt a quick kiss. "No. I can manage that for myself, thank you. I plan on soaking for a while and then I am for bed."

"Alright. I think I will take a stroll while you do that. I might even manage to find Tallee tonight instead of tomorrow. I'll be back in a little while." Brandt said.

When Thomaline had shut herself in the bathing room, Brandt donned his sword belt before leaving the room. Both guards were now in place and Alred had vanished. Maybe it was time to check on the cat. Brandt might find out what had set him off earlier.

CHAPTER SIX

Brandt's stroll did not bring him any closer to finding out what either Alred or Prince Cathos might have been doing. Finding no trace of them, Brandt instead sought out Tallee for the second time that day, to pass along Thomaline's wishes regarding the probable reason for the yaral not bonding with any Skellan elf.

"Have you seen Alred recently?" Brandt asked Tallee after the message had been delivered.

"No My Lord. Not since before the evening meal. Why? What has he done now?" Tallee knew the cat well and also knew the kinds of mischief Alred continually got into. Alred could cause more trouble than all the other yaral combined.

"Nothing that I know of, but that might just mean that it's not been discovered yet." Brandt secretly doubted that would be true. The cat had been upset by Prince Cathos for a reason. He just needed to find out what that reason was.

"When I did see him, it was after the Queen left the meetings. He was with the injured yaral, but he left a while later." Tallee explained.

"What injured yaral? What happened to it?" Brandt did not like to hear of any injuries within the fortress.

"I am not certain. He is blocking me when I try to understand what has happened. That he is afraid is all I can understand from him. He has a wound, but he will recover. It's not too serious, just painful."

"When did this happen?"

"Earlier today I would think. He was limping his way to the barracks when I found him, so I do not know where he had been hurt."

"Is he one of the paired yaral?"

"No. He is young and just arrived a few days ago. I have been getting him used to the barracks and the others in the Brigade. He has just been observing what we are doing, and I was hoping he would find a partner from among the waiting soldiers."

"Do what you can, Tallee, but first show me where you found him. I want to see if I can discover where he was hurt. If I can, then maybe I'll discover who has done this." Brandt had a suspicion but without proof it would just be his word against another's. Or maybe he being prejudiced.

Tallee picked up a lantern and led Brandt away from the soldier and yaral barracks, and away from the training yard.

"It was here My Lord." Tallee indicated a spot beside the archway that led to the stables. "He was leaning against that wall for support when I found him."

Brandt walked closer to the place that Tallee had pointed out and saw blood on the ground.

"I did not have time to look further as I called for help so that I could quickly get the cat back to the barracks for medical treatment. I am sorry, I should have investigated further, but I was then busy with other matters."

"Don't worry Tallee. You're not to blame. I'm glad you were here to help. I'm going to follow this trail and see where it leads. The cat bled enough that I can still see the blood in the dark."

"I'll come with you." Tallee stated. He was not going to let Brandt go off into the dark alone. He knew that Lord Brandt still had his detractors within the fortress. This attack on one of the Queen's cats was a serious offense and only a dangerous person would have done this. Or a stupid one.

Brandt held up his lantern and slowly followed the trail of cat blood back towards the horse stables. Tallee followed, his hand on the hilt of the short sword that hung at his side. Brandt had already eased his sword partway from its sheath in anticipation of any danger that might still linger.

"Here! The trail starts here." Brandt said. He could see where the cat had been injured and also the many hoof and footprints that had mingled with the blood and now obscured the signs.

"There are too many prints now for us to tell who has done this," said Tallee.

"I will ask the stable caretakers tomorrow if they noticed who was in this yard earlier. They must not have seen the attack, but they might remember who was here. When I returned this afternoon, I was at the other end of the yard, but I don't remember seeing anyone else when I arrived. Send for me if you find out more tomorrow. I'll tell the Queen as she will want the culprit dealt with!"

Brandt suddenly wished he could communicate with Alred on a level that would give him the confirmation of his suspicions. He was certain that this was the reason for Alred's actions towards Prince Cathos. The sooner that elf was gone from Goldenspire the better for all concerned!

When he returned to their chambers, Brandt found that Alred had already made his way back and was now sprawled on a rug, sleeping soundly. At least Brandt had his side of the bed but even that did not give him a good night's sleep. Despite his best effort, Brandt tossed and turned restlessly most of the night as he could not put the thoughts of intrigue from his mind. He was sure that Cathos had injured the young yaral and he also kept thinking that somehow, the prince might even have something to do with the River Lord messages.

"Are you sure it was Cathos?" Thomaline asked him the next morning after Brandt had told her of his meeting with Tallee.

"Probably, but I have no actual evidence and Tallee has been unable to get anything from the young yaral. I just have my suspicions and the actions of Alred. We know that he wasn't being playful last night. He was challenging Cathos and didn't care if we were there to see." Alred lay on the bed, watching the royal pair.

"Then we must observe more carefully. I cannot act unless there is proof." Thomaline did not doubt Brandt's suspicions, but Cathos could not be challenged without clear evidence of his transgressions.

"I know. I will alert Tallee to my suspicions and I'll also have him pass along a warning to the members of the Queen's Brigade. I won't be able to mention the prince's name, so we'll just have to wait and see if any other incidents occur." He did not like the thought of more problems and until the Skellan prince left Goldenspire, Brandt would have to stay vigilant.

Thomaline's time the next day was spent drifting between Council committees as the plans for the Skellan resettlement continued. Skith seemed to have matters well in hand and her required input was minimal. Her longest conversation was with Princess Agretha.

"Do you have any major concerns?" Thomaline asked the princess when they found a few quiet moments together.

"Not as such. I am quite surprised and very pleased at how well everything is coming together. Everyone involved in the planning has been so helpful." The princess enthused.

"As are your people. There are some concerns of course, but the joint committees seem to be able to solve issues as they arise. It is quite exciting." Thomaline agreed.

"It is!" said Agretha. "After all the time we were ensconced in those mountains, I never thought that I would be so eager to return to that area."

"I sincerely hope that the move will not dredge up too many traumatic memories for your people, but I do believe that is the best region for you to set up your own governance."

"I agree. It is a large and diverse area, and we will be glad and grateful of the autonomy you are providing." Agretha and Cathos would have authority over the new settlements but under Thomaline's ultimate rule as residents of Goldenfell would also be living there.

"And it is close enough for regular visits." Thomaline smiled as Agretha blushed. "I am sure that many will venture the journey on a regular basis."

"I hope so." Said Agretha. "I must reside with our people, but I do not wish to be separated from my friends here in Goldenspire."

"You will always be welcome to visit but that brings to mind a problem that I think you understand." Thomaline began.

"If you are referring to Cathos, then I do understand to what you are referring. I know that you want him gone from Goldenspire and I know why. I had hoped that our move would keep him occupied for the foreseeable future, but I seem to have little sway with him now." As much as she had plagued Thomaline in the past with her remarks regarding how Thomaline ruled, Agretha had respect for this young Queen and knew that Cathos and his clumsy attempts at attracting her attention had been more than just annoying.

Thomaline tried to put her feelings regarding Prince Cathos as tactfully as she could. "You are correct. I do wish him out of Goldenspire. Cathos has been the source of much discontent, and I am hoping his absence will calm some of the turmoil he has been leaving in his wake. I too, had thought that he would take more of an interest in helping your people make plans for the new settlement."

"He has shown very little interest." Agretha frankly stated as she acknowledged exasperation with her twin brother. "I have tried but he has brushed off my overtures asking for his input. He is often gone from Goldenspire, but I do not know what occupies his time."

"I am sorry to hear that, and I must admit that I have been glad of his absences, but I do wish I knew if he has been stirring up more mischief away from sight."

"He does not confide in me as he once did, but I do know that his ambitions have not waned." Agretha was reluctant to say more. Cathos had often spoken with his twin about his grievance regarding Thomaline's Consort. She knew that he thought that he was more worthy than Brandt to stand at Thomaline's side. She had always been worried by the fact that Cathos could not understand that whether Brandt had been there or not, Cathos would never have had a chance with Thomaline. No matter what his ambitions, Cathos would never be Consort, never mind King.

Thomaline sighed. "For now, I will just have to trust that he will cause no harm, but I am sorry, for I must leave you. I see that General Temor is calling for my attention."

Temor had been searching for Thomaline for some time. Even with the impending departure of the Skellan Elves, he had still been looking into the matter of the River Lord. In recent days he had travelled to some of the border outposts to continue looking for someone that might be sending information to the River Lord.

"My Queen, I have some news to report." He told Thomaline once he had reached her side.

Thomaline looked around at the activity in the room and bade her general to follow her to a quieter spot near her quarters.

"What have you learned?" she asked when the door had been closed against prying eyes and listening ears.

"I spent some time at the southern border outposts, looking for clues. I think I have found something." Temor also took a moment to check that no one else was in the room. "All the messages have appeared when one particular elf was on duty. Someone I do not know."

"How is that possible? I thought you assigned the guard duties personally."

"I did! The guards are posted for weeks at a time and the rotation has been constant as have been the guards. I do not know who this guard is, but he has been attached to that squad from the very beginning."

"How? This makes no sense!" Thomaline began to pace as her mind whirled with possibilities.

"I made the initial duty roster, and the commander of the outposts showed me his written orders and I could see that there had been a change, but I did not make that substitution. One of my selections for guard has had a substitution. This is the guard I do not know. The commander did not question the change as many under his current command were not known to him before this assignment."

"Who is it? What is this person's name?" Thomaline queried.

"The name is Moroth."

"This name is not known to me either. We must find Brandt. Maybe he had heard this name." Brandt's time was often spent in the company of the soldiers and guards of Goldenspire, and he worked with many in Arms Master Greth's training grounds. Maybe Brandt had heard of this elf. Unfortunately, Thomaline's time was most often spent in the company of her Council and dealing with matters of court and the time she spent training with Greth was alone or with only Brandt. She had little time to get to know many of the elves of Goldenspire beyond day-to-day contact within the fortress. To her sorrow, she had to delegate much to her advisors. "Regardless of whether Brandt knows of this individual, what else has raised your suspicions?"

"He has been there when all the messages have been found and he has actually found and presented three to the commander. Also, no one knows where he is from or where he goes between postings. Moroth does not talk about himself and is not inclined to spend time with the other guards." Temor explained. "That and knowing that I never assigned him to the post leaves me to believe that he must be involved in the process of creating or receiving these messages."

"Come. We will look for Brandt together. He might be with Tallee." Thomaline led Temor from the room and headed for the main fortress doors. If she saw Skith along the way, she would have him join them. The news that an unidentified elf was posing as a guard and in such a sensitive duty was beyond troubling.

CHAPTER SEVEN

Brandt was indeed with Tallee. He had wanted to check on the injured yaral and to ask Tallee if he had learned anything from the young cat. Tallee had taken him to see the animal and Brandt was again incensed at what had happened when he saw the long wound that ran along the cat's ribs and flank.

"Do not worry," Tallee told Brandt, "the wound is not deep, but it will scar. He is dealing with shock more than anything else at the moment. I think that is why I have not been able to learn what has happened to him."

As Brandt and Tallee stood looking at the wounded animal, Alred silently joined them and as they watched, Alred leant to nuzzle the younger cat, as if to comfort him. Watching the big cat closely, Brandt soon noticed a change come over the yaral. Alred seemed as if he had decided something but before he could leave the stables, Thomaline, Temor and Skith entered.

"Brandt!" called out Thomaline. "Can you join us?"

Brandt bid goodbye to Tallee and went to Thomaline's side.

"What is it?" he asked.

"Temor has discovered something alarming, and we must all discuss what is to be done." She said, laying a hand on his arm. "Take the others to our rooms so that we have complete privacy. I will join you shortly, after I have spoken with Tallee."

Brandt nodded his acceptance and with Skith and Temor following, he led them towards the fortress doors and the royal chambers. The rooms that he and Thomaline shared included a small meeting room that was rarely used. It must be something extremely important for Thomaline to want to use that room now.

While Brandt led his companions away, Thomaline knelt beside the wounded yaral but addressed her words to Tallee.

"Has he conveyed anything to you?"

"No, My Queen. As I just explained to Lord Brandt, I think he is still suffering from shock, but he is improving. I was going to let him rest for the day and try again tomorrow." Tallee explained.

When Thomaline had arrived, Alred had not left the stable and now he moved up and rubbed his head against Thomaline, causing her to sprawl backwards until Tallee rushed to help her stand.

"Really Alred! Was that necessary?" she admonished the cat as she brushed off her trousers.

Alred paid no attention to her words and rubbed against her legs this time. Again, it was a hard motion and Thomaline nearly stumbled.

"My Queen, I believe he wants something from you."

"Yes, attention!" Thomaline made to shove the cat from her path, but he did not budge.

"No, I do not think so. Pardon me My Queen, but I think he is trying to tell you something."

Thomaline was anxious to return to her apartment and join the others and did not want to deal with her pet's eccentricities.

"He will have to wait. I had just wanted to find Brandt and to check on this youngster. Alred will have to find something else to amuse him."

As if he understood, Alred moved and blocked Thomaline from leaving the stable. This time, Thomaline took a proper look at Alred and saw that there really was something he was trying to convey.

"Tallee? Do you think you can learn what he wants? I must return to the others now." As she moved once more, her progress was again halted as Alred now gave her legs a not so gentle head-butt.

"Please stay." Tallee pleaded. "He wants you to understand. Let me try to see if he will pass his thoughts through me." With that, Tallee knelt beside Alred and looked directly into the cat's eyes. Alred glanced from Tallee to Thomaline and then back again. Finally, he sat and moved his head closer to the elf while Thomaline moved to place her hand on Alred's head.

"I've never tried to communicate with Alred in the past. I did not think he would allow it. He is difficult to read." Tallee said as he moved a little closer and raised his hand to slowly place it next to Thomaline's hand, on Alred's head. The cat narrowed his eyes at Tallee but allowed the touch to continue. "He is upset. It has to do with the wounded yaral." Tallee went quiet for minutes while Thomaline stood and watched. Finally, Tallee removed his hand from Alred and stood before his queen. "He knows who has done this and this is not the first time that an incident such as this has occurred. I could not get a clear picture of what has transpired on other occasions, but I believe it was the same individual involved."

"Could you tell from Alred who it was?" Thomaline wondered if her suspicions were about to be confirmed.

"I believe so, My Queen. Although I would not like to say the name to anyone other than yourself." Tallee admitted in a quiet voice.

"Was it Prince Cathos?" Thomaline asked just as quietly after she had checked to be sure that no one else was nearby and likely to overhear.

"Yes, My Queen. That was what I understood from Alred."

"Do you believe that he knows this for certain or is that just what he thinks?"

"I am sorry, but that is hard to determine. He is very sure of the culprit but how that is, I do not know. He can hardly give proof."

"I cannot deal with this at the moment. I am sorry Tallee, but I have something much more pressing that I must address. I do not take what Alred has conveyed lightly but it must wait." Thomaline made to leave once more but this time, it was Tallee who stopped her.

"My Queen. You must try to make Alred understand. I believe that he will take care of this matter if you do not. At least I believe he will try!"

Thomaline looked down at Alred as the cat stared steadily back in return. She could not allow Alred to make the prince pay for transgressions that he might have committed.

"Tallee. Help me. I must try to make Alred understand, and I need to do so quickly."

Thomaline once again placed her hand on the cat's head as did Tallee and together they pled with the cat to take no action at present. Thomaline further tried to instill the message that she would deal with matters in time but for now, all she wanted Alred to do was keep an eye on the prince. She could not afford strife to build between the Skellan and the Goldenfell Elves as that would jeopardize the co-operation that had developed between the two groups for the upcoming move.

"Do you think he understands?" Thomaline asked Tallee when they had finished.

Tallee looked down at Alred with a wry expression. "I think he does, but whether he will do as you want, I do not know. I would think that his obedience will depend on if there are any future difficulties."

Thomaline sighed at that thought. "Let us hope there are none." She said to Tallee. "Now then Alred. Enough! I must go."

Alred moved from blocking her path and raced away towards the fortress doors. As she followed, she had a couple of ideas for the big cat that might keep him in check and hopefully out of trouble. Prince Cathos trouble, at least.

When Thomaline arrived at her chamber doors, Brandt was leaning against one of them, speaking quietly with one of the guards. When he saw her striding along the corridor, he straightened and asked, "Where have you been?"

"I am sorry. I was delayed dealing with another matter but now we must join the others."

Brandt nodded and opened one of the doors. Once they joined Skith and Temor, Thomaline noticed Alred had inserted himself into the meeting room, although he was lying in a corner.

"Now," began Brandt, "what is so secret and so urgent?"

Thomaline then began to lay out for Skith and Brandt what Temor had learned about the mysterious guardsman and his potential involvement with the River Lord messages.

"Have you heard of the name Moroth?" Thomaline asked Brandt and then Skith.

"No." said Brandt.

Skith thought for fractionally longer before he too, replied in the negative.

"Are you sure that Mendeth never mentioned the name at any time?" Thomaline further queried Skith.

"No. I do not recall that name being spoken by anyone and certainly not Mendeth."

"Do you have a description?" Brandt asked Temor. "What did the commander say?"

"In that the commander was not very helpful. This Moroth was just an average individual. Nothing stood out in description or temperament. Average height and weight, blond hair neatly braided and no visible scars. A quiet individual who rarely interacted with the other guards. He kept to himself and never spoke of himself."

"All the better to remain anonymous!" Thomaline snarled as she gripped the arms of her chair. "He could be anyone!"

"What instructions have you left with the commander?" Skith asked Temor.

"I told him that I need to speak with this Moroth, but I did not say why. Currently he is not on duty on the border. His duty was over just after the last message. He is not due to report for another rotation. That will be in nearly thirty days."

"And in the meantime, we do not know where he has gone." Brandt stated before he had an idea. "Is there anyone here who has an ability that could track this Moroth?"

Temor merely shrugged. "I would have to enquire and that will take time. I do not know of anyone who has such an ability that we can use."

"It is worth a try." Stated Thomaline. "Do your best Temor. It is imperative that we find Moroth. More might be at stake than just messages." The security of all of Goldenfell could be in danger, she thought.

When Skith and Temor left, Thomaline turned to Brandt, "I must get back to the committees and see that the last details are settled. I plan to send craftsmen with the Skellan that are going tomorrow to select sites for new settlements."

"Are you going with them?"

"No. I am leaving those choices to Agretha and Cathos. It will be their new home after all."

"Will he go?" Brandt had his doubts.

"I trust that Agretha will persuade him. If she does not, I will try to put the idea to him in such a way that he cannot refuse." She vowed.

"In that event, I will accompany you. I want to hear more about what will be happening."

When they arrived at the main hall of the fortress, the committees were getting ready to depart as they had wrapped up the final plans. Agretha assured Thomaline and Brandt that Cathos would be accompanying the Skellan contingent the next day and that they planned to be away for a least ten days. The craftsmen and builders that were to join them had given the princess a list of their requirements for what they considered necessary to be able to build sound and sturdy dwellings. The Skellan just had to decide on locations that would match the specifications that they had been given.

With all the formal arrangements made, Thomaline had no wish to spend more time in the dining hall and she and Brandt had a quiet meal in their apartment. Even Alred turned up early and stayed in for the remainder of the evening.

The next morning, the pair stood on the fortress steps, watching as Princess Agretha led her people from the Goldenspire courtyard. Prince Cathos rode with the small contingent of Skellan soldiers that was to accompany the group while the two Goldenspire guides kept to themselves near the rear of the riders but not far from the builders. Their skill would not be needed until later in the day.

As the last rider rode through the gate, Thomaline finally breathed a sigh of relief. She had her home to herself, free of interference for a little while at least. Now she could focus on the problem of the River Lord and his messages.

That thought soon brought a call from one of the sentries. Riders were approaching Goldenspire. When Thomaline descended the steps and strode towards the gates, she met her grandmother leading the riders.

"Ah, Thomaline. Just in time to help me down." Leonde said as she let one of the stable attendants take the reins of her horse. Even though one of her servants had already moved to help, he was dismissed in favor of Thomaline's aide. The servant had no quarrel as he and the others in Leonde's party were now free to seek out their own friends and family for the remainder of her stay in Goldenspire.

"You seem to have brought most of your possessions with you." Brandt observed as he gathered up the bags that the servants had passed down from the horses.

"I thought I might be here for a while, and I wanted my things with me." Leonde responded.

Thomaline thought that the things Leonde wanted to keep had more to do with problem solving than being merely personal possessions. Leonde had scant interest in the latter.

Brandt was of the same opinion. "Do you want me to put everything in your rooms?"

"Not the white bag. I will take that for now." Leonde stated as she took the straps of the bag in her hand. "I will need this." Leonde then looked around the courtyard. "Where is Skith? I wish to speak with him."

"I believe he is in the Council chambers. Do you wish to go there?" Thomaline asked.

"I think we all should." The elderly elf stated and then she went to find Skith. "Hurry up with those bags, Brandt. You too, will need to hear what I have to say."

Brandt looked at Thomaline and shrugged but he quickly left to deposit Leonde's other belongings in her quarters. Thomaline hurried after her grandmother once she had directed one of the guards to find General Temor. She was sure he would be needed as well.

Minutes later, everyone was assembled in the Council chamber, even Alred although he had not been asked. As Brandt was the last to enter, he secured the doors before taking the seat beside Thomaline at the head of the table.

As they watched, Leonde began to lay out the messages that she had been studying for a few days. The messages that had been delivered on behalf of the River Lord.

"I have scrutinized these missives all that I am able," Leonde began, "but I must admit that I could not discern who has sent them. Not definitely. What I can tell you is that whomever this River Lord is, he has never touch ink to these parchments or even held them in his hand."

"Does that mean that there is no River Lord?" Skith asked as he bent to look at the messages again.

"Oh, I think that he does exist, but I doubt that he sent these notes."

"You think that he has directed someone else to do this?" Temor asked.

"Again, I cannot say definitively. He may be only minimally involved."

Thomaline observed her grandmother as she spoke. There was more to this puzzle that Leonde had yet to reveal.

"Tell us. What do you suspect, even if you cannot prove it yet."

Leonde thought how best to present her suspicions before she spoke.

"The messages have not travelled through the Ward barrier. They have been created here in Goldenfell and presented as if they have come from outside lands. I do believe that someone from here had contact with the outside world during the short time that the old Ward was inactive. I also believe that the person or persons responsible for these messages still has the means to create some sort of contact with the other side. The wording of the messages point to that conclusion."

"I am sure that you are correct as I have also made a discovery." Temor spoke before the others could ask any further questions. "Since Thomaline visited with you last, I have learned that there is an imposter among the guards at the portal where these messages have been found. The imposter is involved in this plot, though whether he is working alone on our side of the barrier or with others, I have yet to ascertain.

"This information makes me certain of my previous conclusions. We have a traitor in Goldenfell." Leonde grimly stated.

"I agree." Said Thomaline. "No matter their true intentions or their reasons for betrayal, this traitor has revealed the presence of Goldenfell to whoever it is that styles himself as the 'River Lord'. Now, the Men of the south, along the river, must know with certainty that Goldenfell and we elves, exist!"

"Who has been responsible? Do you know Leonde? Temor has learned that the imposter goes by the name of Moroth, but no one has yet to recognize that name." Brandt spoke as he took Thomaline's hand in his.

"I am sure you know who is suspect Brandt. As does everyone here. I have no doubt that the person responsible for all this is Mendeth."

CHAPTER EIGHT

M endeth! Would that they had seen the last of that problem, Brandt mused. Mendeth had tried for years to removed him from Thomaline's side, even suggesting at one time that Brandt should kill himself for the betterment of Goldenfell! It was only the fact that he was close with Skith and his way of thinking that had kept Mendeth from any reprisals during the years before the Xarlerii threat arose. That was when Mendeth finally overstepped badly enough that Thomaline had no choice be to remove him from her Council. The ouster had driven Mendeth to seek out the Skellan by impersonating one of the elves that had been sent out to scout the land in the north. It was Mendeth's further meddling that had created the problems Thomaline and Brandt still faced with Prince Cathos and his ambitions. Mendeth had lied to the prince by promising that Thomaline was a young queen who was seeking guidance from a strong presence such as Cathos to be her consort or even king. That lie had tainted everything about relations with the royal Skellan ever since the Xarlerii had been defeated.

"I know that he escaped from Goldenspire, but I have not heard of anyone who could have helped Mendeth in that endeavor." Thomaline looked at Temor and Skith in turn as they had previously been tasked to look into that matter.

"I have found no one that could tell me who might have conspired to set Mendeth free." Said Temor.

"Nor I. I do not think anyone from the Skellan were involved." Vowed Skith.

"If he hadn't been with us marching to confront the Xarlerii, I would have suspected Cathos, but that could not have happened." Brandt grudgingly added.

"Yet Mendeth escaped." Thomaline then swore angrily. "With or without help he has disappeared and for the past two years there has been no trace." Thomaline then jumped to her feet and began to pace. Her restless energy for the moment, would not be contained. As she came to a stop by her chair, she asked, "Could he have just escaped on his own? Have we been looking for an accomplice that does not exist?"

Temor gave the matter serious thought before making his reply. "I suppose there could be a slight possibility. Afterall, we were all gone from Goldenspire and camped on the border, waiting for the battle with the Xarlerii. The guards that remained were few and many of those were left behind because they could not have made our journey or been able to effectively fight."

Thomaline had also been one of those to interview the guards that had been on duty when Mendeth had made his escape. At the time, she had sensed no deception from any of those elves.

"Leonde? Do you think that you could learn anything from those guards? I confess that I believed they were truthful in their accounts, but I was newly released from the healers when that occurred, and I could have missed something. Would you try?" Thomaline could not remain still and continued her pacing.

"Yes. I will see to that today, but I would like everyone here to tell me of Mendeth's abilities. That would help me when I speak with those guards. Skith, you knew him best. What can you tell me?" Leonde watched as the head of Thomaline's Council sat in thought.

"I now do not believe that I ever really knew Mendeth. Although he was a counselor for years before Thomaline returned and ascended the throne, I now realize that I know next to nothing of him other than he was usually aligned with me and my advice to King Leyrd."

Knowing that it would not help the discussion, Brandt had to hold himself back from commenting on what a poisonous snake Mendeth had been and the fact that he had had Skith's backing. He doubted that his resentment would ever truly disappear.

Skith then continued, "He had abilities that he rarely demonstrated, but I do recall a few instances. He was a talented mimic and could fool many with his impressions."

"He had a very strong use of glamour as demonstrated when he went to the Skellan." Brandt interjected. "He was able to impersonate the scout that was to use that northern portal."

"Yes, that was an unusually strong use of glamour. I would be interested to know how long he could project that image." Leonde wondered as it was a strong talent indeed to be able to alter one's appearance and for more than a short time.

"He is a killer!" Thomaline had not forgotten what had happened to the scout he had impersonated.

"He also had a creative talent." Skith added.

"What do you mean, creative?" Temor asked. His interactions with Mendeth had been less than anyone else in the room and so knew the least about the former council member.

"He could create small objects." Skith was now remembering something that seemed insignificant at the time. "He made me a small token once. I use it as a paper weight."

"That is very interesting." Said Leonde as she digested that bit of information. "I would like to examine that item."

Skith said that he would have it delivered to her.

"Do not forget that he was able to use the talisman that should have been only activated by our late scout." Temor spoke more forcibly. "That, I believe was a demonstration of great ability."

"This is all very useful." Leonde said. "I will use this information when I question the guards. Temor, will you have them available for later? Are they still in Goldenspire?"

"Yes, My Lady. I will make sure that they are presented to you. Just let me know the time and where you wish to speak with them."

"I think here will do. Please inform them that I wish to speak with them after the noon meal. I will ask Sullan to assist me."

Temor agreed and when Thomaline had no more questions for him, he left to find the guards.

"Do you think he impersonated his way out of prison?" Thomaline asked her grandmother as she finally returned to be seated beside Brandt.

"It is certainly something to think about. If he did not have help from an accomplice, I cannot think of another way he could disappear."

"What about this Moroth?" Skith asked. "Is he Mendeth or an accomplice?"

"I cannot say, but with all this new information and maybe some clue that I learn from his guards, I may be able to find out. This evening I will consult with some of my friends. As they helped me in constructing our new Ward, they might also be able to assist with this Mendeth problem as well."

When the others had left the chamber, Thomaline had resumed her pacing as she thought about this latest development.

"I have made a grave error." She confided to Brandt. "I was just happy not to have to deal with Mendeth after he escaped. Instead, I should have been more wary of future problems he might cause."

"That was not your mistake. At least not yours alone. Skith had the responsibility to determine Mendeth's fate and he didn't do that in a timely manner. It was on his watch that Mendeth escaped. You, and even I could not be faulted as we were preparing to fight the Xarlerii at the time!"

"Yes, but I should have followed up on the situation after I was recovered! If I had, we might not have this problem!" Thomaline's eyes signaled great anger as she stopped to face Brandt.

"It was already too late Thomaline. You had only just been released from the infirmary when the first message arrived! You have been trying to find out who was behind these messages ever since."

Thomaline would not be assuaged by Brandt's logic as with a dismissive wave of her hand, she strode from the room.

It was Brandt's turn to utter a few choice words after she left. He was rarely angry with her, but this was one of the few times. Why could she not see reason? Maybe he could work out some of his frustration in Greth's training yard.

Later that morning when he finally returned to the royal apartments, Brandt was covered in dirt and sweat and more than ready for a bath. He felt as if there were no unbruised spots anywhere on his body! Arms Master Greth had brought in another Master. A Master who was skilled in unarmed hand-to-hand combat. Brandt definitely needed more training in that area!

"What has happened to you?" Thomaline jumped to her feet from the chair beside the ever-present fire in their sitting room. "Has someone attacked you?"

"No." Brandt groaned as he limped past her, on the way to pick up clean clothing. "I was training and Greth has a new master to torment me and show me how much I need to learn."

Thomaline watched as Brandt made his selection and then slowly limped to the bathing room. "Will you be long?" She asked before he could close the door.

Brandt looked at her with mild astonishment. She did not seem overly concerned with his present physical condition and Brandt felt his anger begin to rise. "Yes! Yes, I will! I need to try and soak some of the soreness away. Why?"

"Well, I have been waiting for you to return so that we might eat together in the main hall."

Brandt merely shook his head in disbelief before forcibly closing the door. She was becoming more confusing by the day!

"Will you be joining me?" Thomaline called to him. Silence was her only answer. "What is wrong with him?" she wondered to herself out loud. Not understanding Brandt's mood, Thomaline went to the door and requested that one of the guards ask the kitchen to send a meal for two to her quarters. A meal that might put him in a better mood once he had bathed and eaten.

When Brandt finally crawled from the tub and made his way to the sitting room, Thomaline was patiently waiting for him so that they could dine together.

"Are you hungry?" she asked as he took a seat close to the hearth. The fire was not large but any extra warmth was appreciated. He felt as if all of his muscles were beginning to stiffen up despite the long soak in hot water.

Brandt looked at the meal Thomaline had set before her on the table but could not muster much enthusiasm for food at the moment.

"Maybe in a while. I'm not that hungry right now." He told her.

"Are you sure? I asked Cook to send most of your favorites. I thought that might put you in a better humor."

Brandt looked at Thomaline in askance. Still? He had to carefully choose his words, but it was getting harder to keep his temper in check. He was getting tired of edging around Thomaline's mood swings.

"Thank you. That was thoughtful of you. I'll eat in a while as I'd really just like to relax for a moment." He said as politely as he could muster.

Thomaline said nothing but left the table and moved to a sit on a chair beside Brandt. For the time being, she was content to quietly enjoy watching the dancing flames in the hearth. When hunger drove him and he felt that he could finally move, Brandt limped to the table and placed food on a plate, to carry back to his chair. He would find some way to pay Greth back for this trickery! This new Master, Master Broday, would figure into his plans as well. He was nothing if not willing to learn, but he could not get behind a training lesson that would leave him incapable of defending Thomaline if such a need arose.

"What did you learn from this new Master? Do you think I should learn as well?" Thomaline believed that any training Brandt and her guards received should be shared. She did not like to rely on others to always protect her and her throne.

"Master Broday is just as exacting in his training methods as Master Greth. Maybe even more so. His skill is in unarmed, hand-to-hand combat, not with weapons but using our own strength and agility against other opponents. I think it will be very useful training. I just didn't expect to be doing that today and I had other things on my mind that hurt my concentration. Now I'm paying the price, but I'll be fine by tomorrow." He said. He hoped that would be how he felt. Brandt doubted that he could feel worse.

"I think that I want to try this new training. I will speak with Arms Master Greth to set up a schedule while the Skellan pick out the locations for their new settlements. I might not have time when they return."

"Make the arrangements but be warned; Master Broday will not ease his training methods just because you are Queen."

"I should hope not. I never ask for special consideration."

Brandt knew this was true but still felt that Thomaline did not truly understand the consequence of her wish to train under Master Broday. Oh well. She would learn, just as he had.

When Brandt had finished with the food on his plate, a guard knocked on the door and announced that Leonde had come to call.

Thomaline bade her grandmother enter and offered her a chair near Brandt. At Leonde's questioning look, Brandt gave her a brief account of his training debacle at the hands of Master Broday. Leonde found great mirth with his account.

"From what you have just said, you may not believe this, but Broday was easy with his training. Master Broday also trained Master Greth, so you have had the two most skilled and experienced warriors in all of Goldenfell take you under their guidance. Master Broday does not train anyone now so to have instructed you today, Master Greth must have personally made the request."

"If I didn't feel so bad at the moment, I would probably thank them but that will have to wait."

"Will he train me as well?" Thomaline asked.

"I am sure that he will. If he has come out of retirement to train Brandt, then he will guide you too."

"Retirement? Why is he retired?" Brandt questioned. Master Broday was eminently fit.

"Why should he not enjoy retirement. Master Broday was Arms Master to my husband. I think he has finally learned to relax a little."

That information gave Brandt pause. In his estimation, Leonde was ancient. Master Broday must be of equal age or more if he was Arms Master that long ago. It was very discomforting to realize that he had been so abused by such an elderly trainer!

"I have come to speak with you concerning the Skellan move." Leonde said as she turned to her granddaughter. "I was wondering how long you thought it would take?"

"They have only been gone a few days and so I doubt that they will be back before the new moon. When they return, all those that wish to take part in the building of their new dwellings will be sent with the supplies they require. I would imagine that if everything goes even moderately to plan, they should be in shape to complete the move sometime in the fall. Why?" Thomaline looked to Leonde.

"Nothing of consequence. I wished to know how things would proceed."

Brandt raised an eyebrow to that evasion.

"I also wanted to discuss what I learned from Mendeth's former guards."

"Something new?" Thomaline eagerly asked her grandmother.

"Yes, but it was something that seemed insignificant to them at the time. That was why they did not mention it and it was not until I asked new questions that they remembered."

It as Brandt's turn to question Leonde. "How important is this new information? "

"You will be the judge." Leonde began. "Three days before he disappeared, Mendeth started receiving a regular visitor. It was Councilor Dotha. This was not unusual as Councilor Dotha had questioned Mendeth on several occasions with Skith before that day and although he had his own keys to the storage room where Mendeth was being kept, on those three days Dotha always requested that the guards open the door for him."

"Three days before? Are they sure of the time frame?" Thomaline asked, her forehead wrinkled by a frown. From what she remembered that could not be correct.

"Yes. They are now certain. It was the request to unlock the door that helped them remember."

"Why is that significant?" Brandt asked.

"Three days before Mendeth disappeared, Dotha was not in Goldenspire!" exclaimed Leonde. "He was on a patrol that was sweeping the area for any danger. In fact, he had been gone from Goldenspire for six days by then."

"Then who was visiting Mendeth?" Brandt was confused.

"That is what we must discover." Said Leonde. "I have already informed Skith and Temor of this and they are in the process of speaking to everyone that we know was in Goldenspire at the time. It will be a huge task, but someone must know who was impersonating Dotha."

"I can scarcely believe this! It was difficult enough to believe that Mendeth had such strong glamour abilities but to learn that there was another! This could be a disaster!"

"It has been two years." Brandt reminded them. "We will get to the bottom of this but for now I think we must just carry on. If the co-conspirator is still in Goldenspire, we should not alarm them now as they might disappear for good."

"Yes, you are correct. We will not panic." Thomaline calmed at Brandt's words. "We will tell Skith and Temor to go softly for now. We might learn more that way."

Brandt slowly tried rising from his chair, but his back began to protest the move. Master Broday had tossed him to the ground too many times.

"Oh Brandt! You seem to be getting worse! Let me help." Thomaline cried before placing her hand on his chest, just over his heart. Before he could stop her, Thomaline used one of her strongest abilities. She healed him!

Brandt immediately felt renewed. Nothing hurt!

"Thomaline! You should not have done that! You know how much that depletes your strength." Brandt worried. Thomaline had the rare ability to heal others, but the energy to do so came from her own body.

"Do not worry Brandt. I am fine! I did not use much of my own essence and now you are back to normal. I might have to use this ability more often if you keep training with Master Broday." She laughed as her mood had lightened.

Brandt looked for some sign that Thomaline might be masking how much it had cost her to heal him, but she looked just as she had before. Better even!

"I will be back shortly. I want to catch Masters Greth and Broday to set up that training schedule. And I will speak with Skith and Temor." She said as she walked quickly to the door.

"I cannot believe that." Brandt shook his head as he addressed Leonde. "Did you see? I feel entirely healed. I would have thought that she would feel drained after a healing like that!"

Leonde just laughed. "Do you not know?"

"Know what?" Brandt was baffled.

"Has no one ever discussed elven physiology with you?

"Elven what?" He did not have a clue as to what Leonde was referring to.

"The elven life cycle." Leonde tried to clarify.

"I still don't understand." Brandt replied. This was a subject that had never been discussed with him. Everyone kept assuming that he knew all about his elven heritage and this had kept him in the dark about many things.

"Thomaline has entered into adulthood. Or at least she will in a few more years. That is why her ability to heal has become more powerful. All her abilities will strengthen until she has fully matured, but the mood swings may be just as powerful."

Brandt thought he understood now. No wonder Thomaline had remined him of his sister! "Do you mean to say that she was still considered a child before now?"

"Not a child, but not fully mature. She was in the in-between stage."

"But she's more than seven hundred years old!" Brandt exclaimed. How many and how much would her abilities develop?

"Yes, and she is still very young in elven terms. Now though, the future of Goldenfell might be secure."

"How do you mean?" Brandt asked, still perplexed.

"In a few years, Thomaline will be old enough to maybe conceive a child." Leonde explained. There was something else she needed to explain to Brandt before this last shock took hold. A child!

"You must help her moderate her abilities from now on. She healed you without a thought as to the possible consequences to herself and in other circumstances that might produce a dangerous outcome for Thomaline."

"You mean that she might not know her own strength?"

"Not exactly." Leonde thought about how to explain. "What I mean is that her abilities might be quite volatile until she learns to control power surges in her abilities, not just with her healing abilities but that might be the most dangerous to her. Do not let her try and heal on a whim. It would be best if she had someone else to draw from if she works to heal anyone. She must use a controlled approach in the use of her powers."

"Why are you telling me this?" Brandt cautiously asked.

"I will talk with her as soon as I can. I know that she will be aware of the problems that might arise, but the use of new and stronger abilities is a heady experience. She might need reminding of this from time to time."

Brandt hoped that Thomaline would listen to him if need arose. Being headstrong was a trait he could already see being amplified.

CHAPTER NINE

While still relieved at the revelation of the cause of Thomaline's moodiness, Brandt had to wonder at Leonde's words. She had said that this transitioning would take a few years. He had to speculate as to just how many years. As she was talking about an elven matter, Brandt was afraid that years might take centuries in human terms. He shuddered at the thought. He would have to ask Palin. Palin had been one of Thomaline's companions when she had left Goldenfell after her uncle the king had banished her. He was now one of her councilors and Brandt's best friend. His friend had always been the source of his information since he had come to Goldenfell and now it seemed that Brandt's education had been sorely lacking in an important area. For the time being though, he would have to set that thought aside and find Thomaline. Mendeth was once again the more immediate problem.

He found Thomaline in the courtyard, speaking with General Temor.

"What's happening?" he asked the pair.

"Skith is calling all the councilors to another meeting and Leonde will also join us. We must discover who else had access to Mendeth while he was imprisoned."

"We are starting with the councilors and will expand to others as needed." Temor added.

Thomaline then led them towards the waiting meeting. Brandt had hoped that this time with the Skellan leaders out of Goldenspire and otherwise occupied, would give him and Thomaline some quiet moments together. He had wanted her to relax a bit, if that was possible, but it always seemed that she was forced to deal with one problem after another!

Skith, meanwhile, was wondering how this session should be conducted. It was always possible that one of the council was in conspiracy with Mendeth.

Would having an open meeting be wise? Should they conduct an interrogation of the councilors one at a time? He could scarcely believe that one of that group was working against Thomaline and Goldenfell. As Thomaline entered the room, he hurried towards her. When he very quietly started to explain his concerns, she took his arm and guided him out of the room and into the corridor where Brandt, Temor and Leonde now stood. The guards were send down the corridor to afford the group more privacy.

"Skith has a concern." Thomaline told them and Skith explained his dilemma.

"Have the open meeting." Leonde advised. "If you cannot trust your councilors then that problem must be met now."

"My Queen, your grandmother is correct. For myself, I cannot believe that any of them would betray Goldenfell so let us see what all their reactions are to this information."

Brandt remained silent while Thomaline considered what these advisors had said.

"We will meet together and together we will learn all that we can." She declared and opened the room doors.

As usual, once they were seated, Skith opened the session, but this time his opening statement shocked them all.

"We have a traitor in Goldenspire," he began as he looked at the faces around the council table, "maybe in this very room." It was a dramatic statement that seemed to shock all the councilors and soon angry demands for more information were shouted.

"Quiet! Please! Lord Skith will explain." Thomaline called out above the clamor.

"For two years we have all wondered how Mendeth escaped from Goldenspire and where he is hiding. We now have new information that points to how he could have escaped. Although we still do not know where he might be, it appears that he did have help. Help from someone who might still reside in or near this fortress." Skith could see the indignant looks slowly change to show consideration for his words.

Skith looked directly at Councilor Dotha. "We have learned that while Mendeth was imprisoned and just before his escape that he was visited on several occasions by Dotha."

The councilor in question straightened in his chair as if stung by an accusation.

"We also know that it could not have been Dotha at that time because he was not even in Goldenspire." Skith went on and Dotha relaxed a bit. "Someone with an excellent glamour ability impersonated Dotha to gain access to Mendeth. This is why we believe that Mendeth was assisted by this imposter. What we need to discover, is who among us has this ability and with such a close connection to Mendeth that resulted in his escape."

Immediately, the councilors began speaking over one another, firstly in denial and then with urgent speculation. Thomaline could see that Sullan was trying to follow as many outbursts as possible as she was trying to use her ability to know the truth. Thomaline hoped it would work. She gave Sullan a slight nod to indicate that she understood.

Skith had also witnessed the brief exchange and now called for attention. The questioning would begin.

"Dotha was the one who accompanied me the most when I spoke with Mendeth, and we know that he was not in Goldenspire when the imposter went to see Mendeth." Skith began, but was soon interrupted.

"How do we know with certainty that Dotha was not here?" Questioned one of the older, more querulous councilors. "Maybe it was the imposter that was away from Goldenspire."

It was a solid point, but Skith was still annoyed by the interruption.

"Do you have reason to believe that Dotha would have the ability to do such a thing? Are you aware of something that you should have told this council previously?" Skith asked.

The councilor merely shook his head. That was to be his only input as Skith and Thomaline took turns in asking the other councilors about what they might have witnessed during the time in question. Only one other had accompanied Skith when he saw Mendeth, and no one had seen him alone. Sullan listened carefully to what was said by all. Two of the members had been on the front lines with Thomaline and her army and could offer no information but one the remaining women surprised them.

"I know of no one with such an ability, but I do wonder if it could have been someone young enough to have just come of age. Might that be the reason that we have not heard of this strong ability before now?"

Brandt had not heard of this coming-of-age situation before that day and now it was spoken of twice in the same day! Although the councilor did have a valid point.

"You may very well be correct Maggrid." Agreed Leonde.

"There are not many of the correct age," Temor added, "but of those, some are not known to me as they came to Goldenspire when the army was called up."

"This may be why we never knew of a connection to Mendeth. They only arrived two years ago." Thomaline agreed.

"There is a flaw to that thinking." Brandt then pointed out, "It does not have to be a younger elf as many elves came here for protection when the Ward was about to fail. Many have yet to return to their previous homes."

"Brandt too, is correct, we must still keep open minds. We have not reduced the number of elves that could have been involved. We still need to question many more." Then she had an idea.

"Sullan, would you like to be in charge of a project I have in mind?" Thomaline asked.

"What task My Queen?"

"It might help if you could interview as many as possible under the slight ruse of learning who will definitely want to move to the new Skellan settlements when they are ready. It would be a perfect opportunity to speak to large numbers of our residents and also to ask more pertinent questions of anyone that did not reside here before the Xarlerii threat. Palin can help you find others to assist with this." She explained and smiled at her friend Palin when he nodded his agreement.

Brandt thought this was an inspired idea. The task would be beneficial for planning the upcoming move and also in detecting a traitor. Although many had initially been enthusiastic about leaving for a new home, some had now rethought the idea.

"Of course, My Queen." Sullan agreed and looked to Palin for his consent. "We will start after this meeting."

"Why not wait until tomorrow?" Palin asked. "We can decide upon our most pertinent questions and then ask others to help us. They do no need to know the reason we will be asking questions."

"Good! I will leave it to the pair of you. Report to me, Skith or Temor as soon as you learn anything useful." Thomaline instructed. With that the meeting was soon adjourned although Thomaline asked Sullan to wait while the others departed.

"Did you hear anything untruthful?" she asked Sullan.

"No, My Queen. Thus, I do not suspect that anyone that was present just now helped Mendeth in anyway."

"This is very good news. I could not believe that anyone of my Council would have been in league with Mendeth after his treachery. I have every confidence in your ability to help us seek out who was."

There were still more items on Thomaline's agenda, but finally, Brandt managed to convince her that they had done enough for the day. Their evening meal was held in the apartments were he eventually convinced Thomaline to relax. After their meal, she left the table and sat before the fire in the hearth where she once again stared for some time at the flames waving before her eyes.

"Would you like a cup of wine?" Brandt asked as he poured one for himself.

"Please." She replied and then smiled at him when he passed her a goblet.

"Why don't we go for another ride tomorrow?" Brandt wanted to get her out of Goldenspire for a while. Why not let Skith and Temor handle things for a while?

"I should not. I need to help with discovering who might have aided Mendeth."

"No, you don't." Brandt firmly replied. "You have put people in charge. Let them do their jobs and deal with this and any other issues that might come up. At least let them do so for tomorrow. From the little that Leonde has told me, I think that you need to take more time for yourself right now."

"What exactly did she say? Why are you worried?"

"I always worry. Someone has to worry about you. You never seem to give much consideration for your own wellbeing. You need to do that."

"I am fine Brandt. Do not let Leonde concern you unnecessarily. This is a perfectly natural transition for me as with any other elf. You might find yourself in a similar situation one day." She said with a mischievous grin.

"What! Surely not. I passed puberty many years ago." Brandt was horrified by such a thought.

"You went through human puberty. You might very well experience something equivalent now that your elven ancestry has taken hold. You've only been here for eighty years after all." When she saw his still horrified look, Thomaline relented just a bit. "I doubt very much that you would undergo a physical change, but you really might see an elevation in your elven abilities."

That thought held some appeal for Brandt as he took his chair before the fire, at Thomaline's side.

"Now you've said something that I could look forward to. I hope I don't have to wait hundreds of years for that to happen. What about you? Will this 'maturing' take a long time?"

"Oh, do not look so worried. A year, maybe two or three. That is all, but I am sorry to tell you that those years might make me a bit unpredictable."

That was an understatement! If this past season had been any indication, it might be safer to find more endeavors away from Goldenspire or at least he could find somewhere to hide out from time to time.

"I'll try to be brave in the face of that danger." He laughed now. "Tell me more about the elven life cycle. I had never thought about that until Leonde mentioned it earlier."

The rest of the evening's conversation was a revelations for Brandt as he learned so much about his elven physiology, but there were some personal things about which he still needed to speak with Palin. It was an ongoing mystery as to how much elven blood really coursed through his veins.

The next morning, as Brandt and Thomaline were thundering along a mountain trail, Brandt had to wonder how many days would pass before the Skellan returned to Goldenspire. Preparations were still being made for the move and the creation of new settlements, but he did not want to see Prince Cathos return. If it were not for the search for Mendeth's accomplice, life in Goldenspire would be almost peaceful and that was a condition that they had not seen for a few years now. He wanted to look forward to a time like that again.

When they came to a halt to rest their horses, their talk turned to personal matters until Alred crashed through the brush to join them.

"I thought cats were supposed to be silent hunters." Brandt stated as he gave Alred a sour look.

"He usually is but I think he also likes to make an entrance when he can."

As if he understood, the cat took a moment to preen and casually lick a bit of fur back into place were the brush and trees had mussed a spot. When the pair rode on, Alred kept pace, just to the fore of their trail. Thomaline had taken Brandt's previous night's suggestion to heart. They were all heading to a small waterfall and pool, where Thomaline had decided to go swimming. Although it was now late spring and Brandt knew the water would still be icy cold, Thomaline was determined. She had not told Brandt yet, but there was a new ability she wanted to explore. When they arrived, Brandt looked at the small pool below the little waterfall and could not help but notice the stream that fed it came from high up the mountain. It was pure ice melt!

"I told you it would be too cold!" He exclaimed as undaunted, Thomaline dismounted her horse.

Ignoring Brandt's disapproval, she secured the horse to a nearby tree and began to pull a few items from her saddle bag.

"We have a nice warm bathing chamber at home and plenty of hot water. Why do you want to risk your health by freezing to death in that ice bath?" If he could not dissuade her, he was certainly going to resist joining the insanity.

"You might be surprised if you would just come into the water with me." Thomaline began to disrobe beside the pool. She had brought towels for both of them.

"The only surprise would be if I didn't die of frost bite." He declared. Nonetheless, Brandt also dismounted and secured his horse. Alred had circled the pool and was now standing beside Thomaline. He might watch, but Brandt had never heard that any of the yaral had a fondness for water other than for drinking.

"Come! Please Brandt. I want to show you something new. Join me!" She held out her hand and despite his misgivings, Brandt went to join Thomaline.

"Alright. Give me a moment." He needed to remove his weapons, but he wanted them right beside the pool, in the event that he might need them. Afterall, Goldenfell's Queen was still his to protect.

"Hurry!" Thomaline had left her clothing on the bank and was anxious to get into the water. It was cold standing there waiting for Brandt.

"The things I do for love!" Brandt muttered as his clothing was soon joining hers and he took her hand as she stepped into the pool.

"Is it deep?" Brandt could swim but he did not think he would be able to tread water for long if the water were as cold as it looked.

"Never mind that! Come!" Thomaline pulled harder and Brandt was dragged into the water that now came above his knees.

"Are you trying to kill me?" He exclaimed as the shock of the water hit him, causing his teeth to start chattering.

"Never." She said with a loving smile and then Brandt notice something amazing! The water was now as warm as bath water.

"What did you do?"

"I told you; it is something new. I just discovered it a few days ago. I can warm the water. I barely have to think about it, and it just happens."

"This is amazing." Brandt told her as he followed her deeper into the water. Soon they were both floating in the now warm water. When he turned over and started to swim away, he was in for a nasty surprise. The water was only warm within a few yards of Thomaline.

"I am sorry Brandt." She laughed as he hurriedly swam back to her side. "I guess it only works in my general vicinity." It was her turn to swim away and Brandt was forced to stay by her side or suffer the ice-cold water once again.

After a few more minutes, Brandt suggested that they return to the pool edge where Alred waited.

"This could lead to something that Leonde warned me about." He told Thomaline when she protested leaving. "She said that your abilities could harm you if you used them unchecked. You could easily overextend yourself if you are not careful."

Thomaline did not think that just warming a bit of water would hurt her but finally acceding to Brandt's wishes, climbed out of the pool and handed him his towel.

"I know that you are right but that was fun. I just wanted to see how much I could do."

"I think I understand. It must be quite a heady experience to find out you have a new ability, but you will always be my first concern, and I trust that I will always be here, reminding you to be careful."

"Then you must promise me the same." She admonished.

Alred soon grew bored with the pair and left to hunt before they all returned to the fortress. Brandt and Thomaline did not even notice he was gone.

CHAPTER TEN

Thomaline groaned as she sat up in bed. Brandt pulled the covers over his head and tried to burrow deeper into his pillows.

"Get up!" Thomaline gave his shoulder a hard poke with her finger.

"Why?"

"Agretha and Cathos will be back today."

It was Brandt's turn to groan. Why could they not stay away from Goldenspire for a bit longer? It had been so much pleasanter while the Skellan royals and their party had been gone. Thomaline gave him another poke before slowly climbing from the bed. What she needed was a hot bath. Now!

"Wake me when you're done with the tub." Brandt mumbled. He too needed the relief that might come from a hot bath. Being too stiff and sore to move was another reason for the groans as well as the returning Skellan.

For the last six days, Brandt and Thomaline had been training with both Arms Master Greth and Master Broday. If he thought he had been sorely bruised during his first session with Master Broday, he had been sadly mistaken. The only consolation he had was that Thomaline had been equally abused by the harsh training methods. He kept that thought secret though as she would never have kept on healing him of his aches and pains if he had not. Unfortunately for Thomaline, she had not really mastered the art of healing herself as she had with her ability to heal others. She needed to fully draw on the strength of another to heal her pains.

"No." Thomaline said as she pulled on a robe. "If I am up, so are you."

Alred settled the matter by jumping on the bed and stretching out to his impressive full limit, giving Brandt a hard nudge to the edge of the bed as he did so.

"Besides," Thomaline reminded Brandt, "it is easier to heal your hurts if your muscles are already loosened."

"Alright. I'm up. I'll order breakfast to be sent up while you bathe."

Brandt grabbed his robe and then had to struggle into it as Alred tried to play tug of war with the hem. When he had finally managed to don the robe, Brandt reached for one of the pillows to whack the cat before leaving the bedroom. Ohh! He should not have done that as his back protested the move!

When Thomaline had dressed and left the bathing room, it was Brandt's turn. He was pleased to see that breakfast had been delivered after he too had bathed and dressed.

"Come here!" Thomaline commanded as she pulled Brandt to the chamber door. As soon as the door was opened, a guard reached out a hand that she grasped, and Brandt was almost immediately healed.

"Now, you." Brandt said after he had thanked the guard for his donation to his healing.

"I do not think I can." Thomaline shook her head.

"You won't get better at it unless you keep trying." Brandt was firm. She had to learn to control her healing ability. It could be vital one day.

The other guard cautiously reached out his hand to his Queen. This had been a daily occurrence since the beginning of the extra training sessions. Thomaline sighed but clasped the guard's hand as directed. With Brandt's encouragement she tried healing herself. It was only partially successful, and the guard looked as if he needed to sit down.

"Here, My Queen. Try again with me." Said the first guard.

"I should not. I have already used some of your energy to heal Lord Brandt. Look at your partner! I do not want to do that to you as well."

"My Queen, please try. I will be fine." The guard assured her. And he was. When she took his hand again, her ability to heal was effortless.

"Thank you! I hope that I have not drawn too much from you. Please go and request another set of guards for the remainder of your duty. You both must rest."

The guard agreed to the order and went in search of replacements while Thomaline ushered Alred from the room with instructions to remain with the other guard for the time being. Brandt hoped the cat was in the mood to obey as the remaining guard looked ready to drop.

"I wonder why that happened?"

"What?"

"Why was I able to heal you and myself without a noticeable drain to the first guard, while the second guard looks ready to collapse?"

"I don't know. I suppose that would be another question for Leonde."

Thomaline had been healing them both, every day with assistance from the guards as neither wanted it known how much the training was affecting them. Also, no one was to know the extent of Thomaline's healing power and the guards had all been sworn to secrecy for their part in the exercise.

"I will be sure to ask her. That was the second time that particular guard was able to help me heal and using his essence seems to cost him almost nothing and I have no trouble with my power when he assists."

Brandt concentrated on his breakfast. Thankfully, there would be no training sessions today. Or any day that the Skellan royals were in Goldenspire. They could offer no weakness in the presence of Prince Cathos.

"What are we doing today?" Brandt asked when he had cleaned his plate. "Before the Skellan get back."

"I am going to the barracks to spend some time with Tallee and the yaral. What of you?"

Brandt thought for a few moments and then decided, "I am going to see the armor maker. I have not worked with him for a while, and I don't want to stop that training. I believe that I'm getting quite good now." Like some of his elven and even human forebearers, Brandt had found that he had inherited a talent for the workings of metal and in the making of weapons. His secret wish was to come close to the ability of Skith's father who had made the wonderfully special armor that Thomaline and Brandt both possessed.

"Then I will meet you back here for the noon meal. The Skellan should return early this afternoon."

Thomaline collected Alred from his assignment of assisting the guards on duty at their door and hurried off to meet Tallee.

Brandt, however, was hailed by Leonde before he could make his way to the armorer's huge smithy.

"Brandt. A moment please." Leonde called to him and beckoned him to follow her to her own suite of rooms nearby.

"Yes?"

"The Skellan are back today."

"Yes. Thomaline told me before breakfast." Brandt explained.

"Do not train further with Broday while they are here."

"We're not. We don't want them knowing anything about that." Nor did he want to present his back in a weakened state to the prince.

"Good. Also do not let them learn about Thomaline's increasing abilities."

Brandt was happy that Leonde was concerned but he and Thomaline already had this in hand.

"We plan not to. Our guards have all been sworn to secrecy and I know that Broday and Greth would never say anything." Brandt tried not to show his impatience with Leonde.

Leonde smiled at the thought of those two old friends being questioned by that supercilious prince.

"While I'm here, I have a question." Brandt ventured. He might as well ask Leonde now as there might not be time later. "Thomaline was going to seek you out when she had time, but since I'm already here, I will ask. Thomaline has been having trouble healing herself. It has been an erratic experience as sometimes it works and sometimes it doesn't. It also works better with a few guards than it does with others. Do you know why?"

"This is not my area of expertise and in fact we have few if any healers that can even come close to what Thomaline can accomplish. It is unusual for someone to be able to work a complete healing as Thomaline does. Most can only ease their patients and it is very rare for one to be able to use another's essence in a healing. Maybe those few guards have sympathetic abilities, maybe a latent healing ability of their own. It also may have to do with the type of healing she has been accomplishing."

"What do you mean?"

"Well, she has mainly been healing aches, pains, and bruises not mortal wounds."

"She can hardly do that without letting everyone know how strong her ability is to heal."

"I understand that, but I do wonder what would happen if she tried a more complex healing."

"I hope she doesn't have to try. At least for now. I'd like her control to be better before trying something harder. As I had said, Thomaline says that one of our guards is much easier for her to work with than any of the others and it also appeared to cost him very little of his own strength when she needed to draw from him."

"That is strange. Who is the guard? I would like to speak with him."

"It is Ilan. She has used him several times and he has suffered no ill effect. There was one other who also aided more. It was Staf and she suffered very little, although more that Ilan."

"That is curious. I will seek them out when I have the time. I do wish to learn more about the process from their point of view but for now, try not to let Thomaline attempt a more complicated healing. I wish to be there if she does. I want to learn more about her ability and so I must observe how it is accomplished. It might help me to stop her if she tries something that could injure her health."

Brandt agreed and then left to meet with the armorer. He had lost some of the time he had wished to spend in the smithy.

Thomaline as well had been waylaid on her journey to the barracks and Tallee. Temor had found her and wished to give her an update on his mission to seek out who had assisted Mendeth in his escape.

"Lady Sullan still is attempting to speak with as many of our inhabitants as possible. So far, the ruse has raised few if any questions. Unfortunately, she has not learned much of use." Temor lamented.

"It was to be expected. Unless she speaks with the actual person responsible, I doubt she will learn anything other than who wants to go with the Skellan. We still need to learn how much of our joint population will wish to move." Thomaline hoped the numbers would not be too great for the Goldenfell elves.

"I have questioned most of the guards, but there are two that are not currently in Goldenspire. They are on assignment at the border."

"Which border, Temor. I hope we have not sent them to the south."

"No, My Queen. They are at one of the permanent sites in the northeast. I was going to go there after we find out what the Skellan party have to tell us when they return. If I leave this afternoon, I should be there in a few days."

"Let us hope that it is all good news but for now, I must get to the barracks as I wished to spend some time there and with Tallee."

"Very good, I will see you later. From reports I have received; the prince and princess should be here in the early afternoon."

"Does Skith know this?"

"Yes, he has asked the kitchen to have a later meal prepared for when they arrive."

"If you see Brandt, please tell him as well. We might as well wait for them to arrive and then all can dine together."

With a nod of acknowledgement, Temor gave a small bow and left to do as Thomaline wished.

Thomaline was heartened by the notion of the Skellan's later arrival. It would give her more time with Tallee and the yaral and she would still have time to clean up before Agretha and Cathos arrived.

The first thing Thomaline wanted to do was to check on the young yaral that had been injured some days back.

When she found him, Tallee was sitting on a stool in the barracks of the Queen's Brigade, apparently in communication with that very cat. At her entrance, he removed his hand from the cat's neck and stood to greet her.

"My Queen, how may I help?"

"I just wanted to spend some time among the yaral this morning and check on this one. How is he coming along?"

"He is healing, and I think I am making progress in gaining his trust. At least he is not just thinking of returning to the mountains."

Thomaline considered this and then carefully knelt near the cat. When it did not immediately pull away, she slowly held out her hand and tried using her small ability that she used to communicate with animals. The cat's eyes widened at the contact but leaned forward so that Thomaline's hand made a firmer contact with its head.

Thomaline nearly fell to the ground. She could clearly see the cat's thoughts!

"What is it?" Tallee immediately realized that something unusual had happened.

"I can understand him!"

"What do you mean? How? What is different?" Tallee and Thomaline had both worked with yaral in the past and it was Tallee's talent that held the greater sway. Thomaline had always been able to comfort and quiet animals, but it had been a struggle to understand them with any degree of accuracy.

"It is amazing! I can see the pictures from his mind and actually understand some of what he is trying to tell me!" Slowly she removed her hand from the cat to see if the connection remained. "Oh! That is disappointing."

"What?" Tallee was anxious to know.

"I appears that I must remain in physical contact with the yaral to understand him."

"What was he trying to tell you?"

"His thoughts were shown to me as images. Is that how you communicate with them?"

"Yes. I find that it takes a while to sort the images into some kind of order that I can understand as they are jumbled somewhat."

"Yes. That is what I saw. I need a moment to do as you say. It is like sorting out puzzle pieces as a cat's perspectives are different than ours."

Tallee agreed. "That is a most apt description, My Queen. Before you arrived, I learned that his wound has mostly healed and no longer troubles him and that his fear of those of us that live in this fortress have receded somewhat."

"Yes. He feels safe here with you. How is he with others?"

"He has kept away from most of the soldiers. There are only two here that he has allowed to approach him and then, only when Alred is with him."

It was then that Thomaline realized that Alred had not followed her to the barracks. Somewhere along the way, her cat had left to pursue his own interests.

"It is well that he has progressed this much. I hope that I can communicate just as well with the other cats as I have with this one." Thomaline wanted to seek out any other yaral that were nearby and rose to go with Tallee. The young cat had other ideas and yowled for her attention.

"Try again My Queen. I do not think he finished what he was trying to tell you." Tallee came back to stand near the yaral as Thomaline again placed her hand on the animal.

Once more, Thomaline was flooded with images, but this time had no trouble sorting them into a meaningful message. They were all to do with one person. Cathos!

"That vile idiot!" Thomaline was instantly in a rage, and it was Tallee's eyes that widened at the next flow of words from his queen. His soldiers would have been impressed by her imagination and eloquence!

When she was once again in control of her rage, Thomaline informed Tallee what the young yaral had shown her. Cathos had deliberately sought out a yaral and this one had been the cat he had cornered. From what Thomaline had seen, if the yaral had not been so agile, Cathos would have killed it with his attack. No wonder Alred had challenged the prince. He must have learned what had happened from this youngster.

"He may not have been the first to suffer from Cathos's treatment." Tallee ventured as he recalled previous agitation among his charges. Why had they not conveyed a message to him?

"Come with me! I want to see what all the other yaral will tell me."

Tallee followed, all the while wondering what would happen when the Skellan returned in a few hours. He also had to wonder at Thomaline's improved ability to communicate with the yaral. It had certainly been a recent development.

"Have you tried speaking with Alred?" he asked as they entered a large area where many of the cats preferred to sleep during the day.

"No. I just discovered that I had improved in communication when I touched your cat." The young yaral had followed them but now sought out a perch of his own where he could nap.

"I will try later." She vowed. She also wanted to see if her ability would now work on other animals. She would go to her horse before returning to clean up for the delayed meal.

Thomaline approached one cat after the other. Most were not impressed to be woken at that time of day and few wanted to be part of her experiment. Those cats, Tallee explained, were all were paired with soldiers of the Queens Brigade. Only a few unmatched cats offered up any images and they seemed reluctant to do so.

After discussing the matter further with Tallee, they concluded that her ability worked best with unpaired animals and then only when they had something they wanted to impart. Cats being cats, would only co-operate when then wished! She would definitely have to see what Alred could tell her!

Brandt's time had been more uneventful but just as satisfying. His work on a new sword was progressing well and had earned praise from the master armorer. When he finally returned to their rooms, Brandt found that

Thomaline was not changed and was instead attempting to force Alred into communication.

"Has something happened?" he asked as he warily passed the pair. Alred looked stubborn and his tail lashed angrily. Thomaline was clearly exasperated.

"He will not co-operate!" she exclaimed as she suddenly straightened and stomped to her clothes wardrobe.

"What's he supposed to be co-operating about?"

"I was with Tallee earlier and unexpectedly found that I can now talk with the yaral." After observing Brandt's raised eyebrows, she tried to clarify. "Tallee had been working with the young yaral that had been hurt and I wanted to try doing the same. It was a resounding success! I have never had an experience like that before. I was able to see the images that the cat projected just as Tallee has been able to do, but I found some limitations." She had also discovered that her enhanced ability worked better with yaral than horses. Her horse had also been unimpressed with her attempt to discover his thoughts.

Brandt did not see that as a problem. Thomaline seemed to be learning new things and, in his estimation, too quickly. She would exhaust herself at this rate.

"The paired cats do not want to communicate with me, and the others had nothing to say. I wanted to see what Alred would tell me!" she said as she slammed the wardrobe door.

"What were you asking him?"

"I wanted to find out what he knew about that young yaral being hurt. I wanted to see if he would confirm what I learned when Tallee had questioned him a while back. He would tell me nothing!"

Brandt was not surprised, Alred was always difficult and only obeyed when he felt he needed to. Or when Leonde made him.

"What did you learn? Why did you need confirmation."

"I wanted to be sure before I officially banished Cathos from Goldenspire! The cat was attacked by Cathos, and I do not think that was the first time the prince has done something like that. I was trying to find out if he had been seen by any of the other cats."

CHAPTER ELEVEN

When Brandt and Thomaline reached the courtyard, it was already full of the returning party led by Princess Agretha. At their appearance, Agretha immediately left the group and approached Thomaline. They could see the concern on the face of the princess.

"Is Cathos here?" she anxiously asked Thomaline before looking to Brandt.

"I do not believe so," Thomaline replied. "but we have only just left our rooms. I can ask the guards and sentries."

"Please ask. I do not know what has become of him." Agretha turned to survey the courtyard looking for her wayward twin.

"Why are you so concerned?" Brandt asked, not that he really cared if the prince ever returned.

"He left us yesterday. He took two of our soldiers and said that he wanted to hunt but they never returned."

"I still don't understand the worry." Brandt looked to Thomaline. She seemed just as perplexed.

"I am sorry. I know that I am not making much sense, but I do not know why it was such a sudden decision. We were almost back to Goldenspire."

"You do not think he went hunting, do you?" Thomaline could see that was what was concerning the princess.

"No, I do not. He had been quieter than usual on the return journey but would not tell me what he was thinking. Just before he left, one of our soldiers came to him and they had a long talk. They were at the back of our group and at first, I did not think anything might be wrong. Then Cathos called to another soldier, and they rode away with him. Cathos just shouted to me to say they were going hunting and left."

"What made you suspect that something must now be wrong?" Asked Thomaline.

"He made it sound as if they would not be long. I thought the first soldier must have spotted some interesting game. It was not until late last night and they had not returned that I realized they had not taken any bows or spears. All they had were their swords."

By this time, Skith had joined them on the courtyard steps and had heard the last of Agretha's words.

"What would you like us to do?" he asked Agretha.

"I do not know. Not at this time. He is a skilled hunter and warrior, and he has two of our people for guards. I know that he can more than take care of himself, but I still worry. He has been acting secretive lately and will not confide in me as he once did. I also have this feeling that comes from our link as twins. He is either planning harm or has come to it!" Agretha's anxiety was not diminished and Skith reached out to clasp her hands.

Brandt knew which option he preferred. Prince Cathos was up to something, and it undoubtedly involved Thomaline and Goldenfell.

"Come. Let us retire to one of the audience chambers. I will ask for food to be brought as we were waiting for your arrival. We can talk more about this development. Let your people know that a meal is waiting for them in the main hall."

Thomaline beckoned for one of the waiting servants to send word of the change to the kitchens while Agretha went to speak with one of her companions. When that was accomplished, the small group walked up the steps to where Temor now waited. Soon they were all seated in the small chamber. Other than Brandt, no one's appetite was much in evidence.

When Temor had been brought up to date on the situation regarding Prince Cathos, Thomaline changed the subject by asking Agretha how the search for suitable locations for new settlements had progress.

Agretha, momentarily pushing aside her concern for her brother, became more animated. "We have found just what we wanted! There is an area near the mountains that will provide all the timber required to build and has a plentiful water supply and there is abundant game in the area. At least for now. There are potential fields for crops and forage for livestock and there are already wild herds of horses and cattle. The scouts that you sent to guide us found the perfect spot for our new home!"

Thomaline was pleased that at least that part of her plan for the Skellan had worked out.

"We think we have everything ready for when you want to send out the workers to the site. Between our craftsmen and yours, I am sure that you will have a habitable settlement before winter, and I am also sure there will be a steady supply of volunteers." Skith assured the princess.

"That is excellent. I want to send them back right away."

Thomaline promised that the work train would be able to leave the day after next. Now that Agretha had decided upon the site for her new home it was a relief to hear that logs and other timber would not be requiring transport to the area.

Agretha now became graver of countenance. "This is another reason why I am so concerned about Cathos leaving when he did. I assumed that he would stay and oversee the construction of our settlement. I cannot believe that he would just leave this all to me. We had discussed which responsibilities we would each undertake! I was sure that he was just as excited at this opportunity as myself."

Brandt had to wonder about the prince's supposed enthusiasm. He doubted very much that Cathos would be happy that far away from Goldenspire and especially Thomaline.

"I will assist you as my duties allow." Promised Skith. "I also know one of the craftsmen that Thomaline has promised to lead your project, and you can have complete faith in him. When we are finished here, I will take you to meet him and then help you organized the party that will leave for the site."

With their meal now finished, Thomaline probed Agretha for more information about her plans for the new settlement. "Before you go with Skith to talk with Bergo, we should talk with those in charge of learning about who will wish to live in your new community. Some have changed their minds since we first announced this endeavor, and you will need to know the number of settlers that are planning to move and live under your leadership."

"I have become so caught up in the planning process that I have not considered the numbers. Yes! We must do so immediately!" Agretha rose suddenly and started from the room.

"I will be with you shortly," Thomaline called, "I need to have a word with Skith first."

Agretha barely paused but nodded in agreement before she rushed from the room. She needed to find her second in command.

"I don't like it!" Brandt exclaimed after the door had closed behind the princess. "Why would Cathos suddenly leave just before coming back to Goldenspire?"

"I would assume that he is furthering a plan for something I will not like." Thomaline mused. "I knew that getting rid of that nuisance would never be easy."

"He is more than a nuisance." Declared Brandt. "He is dangerous! He thinks nothing of others and is only aware of his own wants and desires." And Brandt knew that Cathos desired Thomaline most of all!

"I was prepared to banish him as soon as he arrived but that will have to wait for him to appear." Thomaline then set about explaining what she had learned about the part that the prince had played in the wounding of the young yaral.

Temor was incensed and Skith's anger was apparent by the grim set of his mouth. That act of senseless cruelty further exposed the prince's lack of character.

"Will you tell Agretha?" Skith asked.

"Yes. As soon as she gets her plans underway for the start of her new home. Maybe Cathos will turn up before then, but I will not wait long. Temor, have the guards beware of the prince's return and instruct that he not be admitted into Goldenspire without my express permission. Make sure that everyone is wary of any attempt by him at a stealthy return. Him or his guards." It was Thomaline's turn to rise and leave. She needed to find Agretha.

As Skith and Temor left their chairs, Brandt said, "We need to increase our efforts to find out who was helping Mendeth. I can't help but believe that he, Cathos and this River Lord are all connected and that they plot against Thomaline and myself."

Temor agreed with Brandt and said he would report back as soon as he returned from the outer guard post where he believed the two unquestioned guards were stationed.

"Be sure that you do not travel alone." Brandt advised. "With Cathos unaccounted for, be extra cautious."

When Temor left, Brandt was alone with Skith. "You look troubled. What is it?" he asked his great-grandfather.

"This whole mess! Mendeth! Cathos! The River Lord! I agree that it would be too large a coincidence if they were not all bound together in something. I just wish I knew what! I would like to help Agretha, but my first priority is to Thomaline and Goldenfell. I do not know where to begin in untangling this mess."

"There is nothing that cannot wait for now. Why don't you go and help Agretha as you promised? She will need your support right now. She has to shoulder all the responsibility for her people now that Cathos has run off. Although she fears that something has happened to him rather than wanting to believe that he's just following some agenda of his own."

"Yes. You are correct. I will go to help her now."

Brandt wanted to consult with Leonde. They had not included her in this discussion, and he wanted to keep her apprised of the latest developments. Through her own sources, she undoubtedly knew things that they did not.

Brandt found Leonde in another of the small meeting rooms near the council chamber where she was in discussion with several of her contemporaries. These were the elves that had helped her construct the Ward that now protected Goldenfell. He waited for a lull in their discussion before asking to speak with Leonde.

"We are finished our talks," she said as the rest of the group rose and left the room, "sit down Brandt."

"I think we may have another problem." He told her as he sat near her. "The Skellan have returned but they are missing a few of their number."

It was Leonde's turn to sigh, as she correctly guessed who was missing.

"Yes," Brandt agreed, "it's Cathos. Agretha is very worried. She says he had a hurried talk with one of his soldiers and then they and another soldier suddenly left using a feeble excuse of going hunting. Even Agretha eventually saw through that ruse. They were only a day away from here, but they haven't returned, and his sister has acknowledged that he may be plotting something."

Brandt's feelings were clear by the look on his face and Leonde was in agreement with him. "As you must also think, I am confident that this sudden disappearance involves some plot." Leonde said while frowning about something.

"I'm sure of it. I also think this must involve Mendeth and the River Lord. I don't know how this is all connected, but I intend to find out. Maybe when Temor gets back, he will have some answers."

"Where has he gone?"

"Two of the guards who had been on duty when Mendeth escaped are not in Goldenspire. They are at a border outpost and Temor has gone to speak with them. They were not Mendeth's prison guards, but they were on duty around the fortress during the time he was a prisoner. We know that everyone else has already been questioned again but with our recent insight into clandestine visits by the false Dotha, he wanted to question those two. He told me after our meeting that he had already spoken to all the other guards."

"What about Thomaline?" Leonde asked.

"She's with Agretha. They want to send out the wagons and workers the day after tomorrow. Agretha says they have found an ideal spot, and she wants to have the construction started as soon as possible. Before they do that however, they need a firm idea of how many will be re-locating as they need to plan the settlement quickly."

"I would like to join them. Do you know where they are."

"Come with me and we'll look. I would imagine that they are in the courtyard somewhere. Thomaline has promised to help Agretha as Cathos now seems to have abandoned her and the project."

"His 'project' has merely morphed into a plan that I suspect he has been plotting for a long time."

He agreed with Leonde's assessment and went with her in search of Thomaline and Agretha. They found the pair seated at a small table that had been set out in the large courtyard and a scribe was busily writing notes from the talks. Around them were representatives of both Goldenspire and the Skellan elves. As Leonde wished to listen to the conversations and not interrupt, they stood behind the pair of royals to observe. The committee members who had been in charge of identifying those who wanted to settle the new community had been competent and thorough and the discussion was swift. Before long, the representatives had finished their reports and Brandt and Leonde approached Thomaline as Agretha left to join her advisors.

"We have a rough tally, and it is a little surprising." Thomaline told them when Leonde had helped herself to Agretha's chair. As the scribe had also left, Brandt too, took a seat.

"What is surprising?" asked Leonde.

"As you know, when the Skellan first moved here, there were around five thousand of their people although nearly five hundred of their soldiers were lost in the battle with the Xarlerii. Now most of their people live in the surrounding areas and have made homes within our settlements. Even with that, I had thought that most would want to move and live with their leaders. I was wrong. Unless some change their mind once again, only about two thousand want to leave and some of those are our own people that have formed unions with some of the Skellan."

"How did Agretha take this news?" Brandt wanted to know. Agretha had not appeared upset when she left.

"Although she tried to hide it, I believe she was surprised as well. The committee leaders had asked why those that are choosing to stay, made that decision. It seems to have come down to stability. Most of those that are not leaving have bitter memories of being driven from their own lands and then of the hardships they endured living in the mountains. They believe that they have finally found comfort and safety here and do not wish to give up what they have found. Those that are moving are younger and a good many of them are soldiers and so appear to be more adventuresome."

"That does make sense. The young are often more bold, and the soldiers need something to keep them busy. After the settlement is built, those soldiers will be the hunters and farmers again or whatever they had been before their wars."

"The remaining elves are happy to continue living under your rule?" Brandt wondered why.

"One representative was quite blunt on the subject. They are not confident in their rulers. Or rather they do not want to be ruled by Cathos. They would rather stay here under my leadership that suffer him." Thomaline related but held back the exact words used.

"I wonder if they will change their minds if only Agretha were to rule?" Brandt mused.

"I think that might spark more discussion. I do not believe they have any real objection to following her." Thomaline hoped that would be the prevailing thought.

"I wonder what the soldiers actually think. Would they support Agretha or Cathos if the issue arose?" Leonde did not believe Cathos would willingly abdicated his rule. His ambition had been clear to her no matter how he tried to hide what he wanted.

"I doubt that all those elves were hunters and farmers in their previous lives. They were probably always soldiers and most soldiers want action. I will try and speak to Agretha about the subject of her brother and her people's loyalty, but I will have to do so with care. That will be a delicate conversation." Thomaline reasoned.

"Is Agretha going with the builders?" Brandt asked.

"No. She has appointed one of her people to lead her group. As we are suppling this mission, I am also sending someone who will be in overall charge of the craftsmen, and we will both be sending messengers that will carry directives between here and the new settlement." Thomaline explained.

"How many are going?" asked Brandt.

"Now that we have a better idea of how many dwellings will be needed, we are sending an initial two hundred to work there. Of those that will be relocating, many wish to travel to the site as soon as they can and build their own homes. Agretha thinks that they should relocate in another month once the initial development has taken place."

"When will Agretha return to the site?" Leonde asked.

"She thinks she will leave Goldenspire when her dwelling has been completed. It is the first that will be built, and the rest of the community will be built around it. I am sure that she wants to stay here as long as she can until we know what has become of Cathos."

"He's only been gone for a day, and he might try to ride in at any time!" Brandt exclaimed. What had Agretha not told them to have such worry about her brother?

"If he tries, the guards have their instructions. He will not be allowed admittance." Thomaline was adamant in that regard.

"Does Agretha know this?" asked Leonde.

"She will. I wanted to let her get this afternoon's session out of the way. I intend to speak with her tonight." Thomaline was not looking forward to that conversation.

CHAPTER TWELVE

Agretha had not been pleased with Thomaline's decision but knew she could not contest the order. Cathos had brought this upon himself, and he would just have to deal with the consequences. There was little time to dwell on her brother's defection at the moment, for now she had to finish organizing the building plans for her new home.

Thomaline had stayed well away from those plans. The new dwelling site had nothing to do with her or Brandt other than lending the Skellan party Goldenspire's chief architect. She had been more than pleased to be consulted as her services had not been greatly utilized in centuries.

When the time finally came to see the group set off for the north, Agretha wished she were going with them but for now she was content to stay in Goldenspire and spend time with Skith. They needed to try and sort out exactly where their relationship was headed.

Skith joined her on the fortress rampart by the secondary gate. This was the gate from which the wagons had departed, and she could still see them in the distance, slowly wending their way along the trail.

"You wanted to go." Skith quietly stated.

"Yes. I am not really needed here but I thought I should wait to see if there is going to be any word from my brother." Agretha looked up at Skith. "I will only wait so long. If I have heard nothing by the next moon, I am leaving. The builders should have some sort of accommodation for me by then."

"You know that I cannot abandon my duties, but if there is nothing pressing that requires my attention, I will escort you."

"I would like that." Agretha said and she could see that Skith was serious with his offer, but she knew that there was always some matter or other that would require his attention and that he would not be able to leave the fortress for long. That was not even considering what madness Cathos might be in the process of creating. Where could he be?

The question went unanswered as the days passed. The princess moped about unless she was with Skith or was engaged by Thomaline. She was counting the days until she could leave and find work at the new settlement that could occupy her time.

"What are you planning to call your new home?" Brandt asked one evening as the meal progressed.

Agretha look puzzled for a moment but then threw back her head and laughed. "Do you know that I have not even considered that question. I am afraid that I have been thinking of Cathos and feeling rather sorry for myself instead. Thank you, Brandt! That was a very good question. One that I will answer as soon as I can." She still had her advisors, and she would put the question to them the next day.

Thomaline too, laughed along with Agretha. She was happy to see the princess jolted out of her doldrums even if it might not last. Later, in their rooms she said to Brandt, "You made Agretha happy. I just hope having even one small task will give her a boost. Maybe now she will get back to managing more details of their move."

Brandt just smiled before he said, "I was hoping for a session at the forge tomorrow. What about you?"

"Oh, must you? I was hoping for a ride through the mountains. It has been days, and the horses must be getting restless again."

"Do you think that's wise? Cathos could be anywhere and planning who knows what. If we must go I think we should take an armed escort."

"I was not planning any activities that needed observing." She laughed.

Brandt smiled at the comment, "It may only be for a few days. I had hoped that Temor would have returned by now with some news."

"He should have been back days ago. I have been concerned but Skith says to give him a little more time. After all, he had a squad of soldiers to accompany him."

Brandt just shrugged and went to open their door. Alred had been scratching to be let in but when Brandt saw who was with the cat, he just stared and then looked in askance to the guards.

"I am sorry My Lord. He just followed Alred."

"Thomaline! You need to see this."

"What?" She asked as she came to the door. "What is he doing here?"

Brandt did not have the answer, but Alred looked as if he did. Behind Alred was the young yaral that Prince Cathos had attacked and injured.

While Brandt and Thomaline watched, Alred led the other yaral into their apartment.

"Wait right there!" Brandt called before he passed the pair and quickly shut their bedroom door. Was this new cat even house broken?

"Alred, who is you new friend?" Thomaline asked. Alred walked to the hearth and lay down while the younger cat looked curiously around at his surroundings before he began a more thorough inspection.

"Why don't you ask him?" Brandt said as he watched the yaral. She was the one that could communicate with animals after all.

"I will. Let him settle first."

Brandt thought the cat looked quite settled as he watched the animal sit near Alred.

Thomaline approached both cats and then reached down to touch the new cat's head. She removed her hand and then tried again. There were no images!

"I am not getting anything!"

"I thought you could see their thoughts."

"I can! I have! These yaral can be so stubborn." She grumpily took her hand away from the cat once more and crossed the room to Brandt. "I cannot read thoughts if they do not send me any!"

"I wonder why Alred brought him here. Try to read him instead."

Thomaline grumbled but returned to the hearth and placed her hand on Alred. This time she was rewarded with images.

By the look of wonder on Thomaline's face, Brandt knew that she had received some communication from her pet. "What did you see?"

"Come here. I want to see how this new animal reacts to you."

"Why?" Brandt was wary of anything that Alred might have devised. He had been ambushed by too many of Alred's 'jokes'.

"Just come here!" Thomaline pleaded and then she stood and beckoned for Alred to leave the hearth and join her.

Brandt approached the young yaral and stood waiting for something to happen. The 'something' was not at all what he expected. The cat suddenly sprang up on his hind legs and placing his paws on Brandt's shoulders, proceeded to lick the side of Brandt's bearded face.

"What is he doing?" Brandt tried to push the cat and his rough tongue away, but instead the animal hooked some of his claws into his shirt. "Ow! Stop that. That hurts!" The claws had passed through the clothing and into skin. "Why is he doing this?" Brandt demanded as he tried to disengage the claws.

"I think he has made a choice."

"What choice? What is going on?" Brandt impatiently demanded as he finally became untangled.

"He has chosen you for his partner."

"His partner? What partner? I thought he was here to pair with a soldier for the Queen's Brigade. I don't need a partner!"

"Whether you need one or not, I think one has found you. That is what Alred was showing me. This cat has found no one that he wishes to partner with among the soldiers. Alred seems to think that as he is mine, you should have a yaral of your own."

"I don't need a yaral. I share Alred and that more than enough cats!"

"Oh Brandt. Just look at him! He has chosen you and you should be honored. Do you know how many soldiers are waiting and hoping to be chosen whenever new yaral come from the mountains? There is a bond now whether you want him or not. You must keep him."

"Keep him where? It might get a little crowded in these rooms."

"One more will not make much difference. Sit with him for a while and explore the bond. I will take Alred into the bedroom."

Brandt shuddered at the thought of what disasters these two yaral could create in the fortress, especially with Alred leading the way. Nonetheless, he brought a chair near the hearth and called to the cat. It came and began rubbing its face over Brandt's boots and trousers. He was definitely being marked by the cat. It looked like he was to belong to the yaral and not the other way around. Soon the cat stopped rubbing and stood up with his paws on Brandt's legs, and a loud and rumbling purr emanated from the yaral's throat while Brandt began to stroke the thick fur of the cat's neck.

"Well, if you're going to be staying, I guess you will need a name. Do you have a preference." Brandt was joking but as he started to reel off choices, some serious contenders, some not, the yaral suddenly yowled at one of them.

"Huh. Is that it? Is that your name?" Brandt asked but the cat just sat back on the floor. "Okay. I guess that's it. Come on Thrad. Let's take a walk outside and try and set a few ground rules." Brandt was not just going for a walk; he was going to see Tallee. Maybe he could explain what had just happened and tell Brandt what he could expect as a yaral's partner. After telling Thomaline where he was going, Brandt called for his new companion to follow and then they both made their way out to the courtyard and then to the yaral barracks. He would have to remember to tell their guards that Thrad was now a new member of the family.

"Tallee! Are you here?" Brandt called upon entering the building. Tallee had moved to new quarters in the barracks when the Queen Brigade has been formed. The thought had been that he would be better positioned to oversee and control the cats. Unfortunately, he had experienced limited success whenever Alred had become involved. Thankfully once the cats had been paired, some of the worst nocturnal activities had ceased. It had been up to the elves that had paired with the yaral to control their animals. General Temor had assumed oversite then. Tallee usually had a small number of yaral to look after as they did not quickly find partners. They were highly selective.

"Tallee?"

"I am here. What is it, My Lord?"

"I need to talk with you." Brandt told the elf. Tallee was pulling on a shirt as he approached Brandt. "Did I get you out of bed?" He had not realized that it was this late.

"I was not asleep." Tallee ran his hand through his unbound hair to put it into some kind of order. "How may I help, My Lord?"

"I'm sorry Tallee. I didn't realize the time, but I really do need to ask you about this." Brandt gestured towards Thrad who was sitting beside his right leg.

"What had he done?" Tallee was puzzled. "He is a very quiet animal and has not left the barracks since he was hurt."

"Well, he left with Alred." Brandt began and Tallee quickly looked around for the Queen's principle troublemaker. "No. He's not here. He's with Thomaline. Give me a moment and I'll try to explain."

"Then come with me, My Lord," and Tallee led Brandt and the cat to his own quarters. It was the first time Brandt had ever seen Tallee's private quarters as they usually just met in the main barrack building. Tallee offered Brandt a chair and both sat at a small table. Thrad began to walk around, sniffing the strange area.

"Now, what can I do for you?"

"A little while ago, Alred showed up at our door with this yaral." Brandt gestured towards the animal. "When I opened our door, in they came, as bold as can be. Thomaline could see that something was about to happen, but she could not get a reading from this one."

"Yes, he is difficult. They all are really. If they do not want to communicate there is nothing I can do to encourage them, and the Queen cannot get through either."

"Well, she go through to Alred! I don't know what he showed her exactly, but this guy has clearly let me know what he wants, and I didn't have be able to read him."

"Now I am intrigued. What?"

"He wanted a partner! I just don't know if this was Alred's idea or his, but it appears that he has claimed me and now I don't think I can get rid of him."

"Partner! He never showed any sign of accepting a partner from the soldiers that were looking. I thought that it was because he was too young. He is actually quite a bit younger than the yaral that usually come in from the mountains. Are you sure?"

"Thomaline is sure, and he won't leave me. He has even pick out a name?"

"A name? How? The other yaral have not done so. At least I do not think they have. They have just been given names by their soldiers."

"I just started listing off names as kind of a joke until I said one that he appeared to like. He started yowling when I said it and now he answers to it." Brandt then called to the cat, using its new name. Thrad just looked at Brandt and then continued his inquisitive exploration of the room.

"I think he must be related to Alred." Brandt grumped and Tallee laughed.

"You should be used to this. He is a yaral after all. Of course, you could be correct about his parentage. He is a little strange compared to the others that reside here."

"Yeah, I have a defective one." Brandt said, but with a smile. Thrad meanwhile had finished his exploration and now joined Brandt. He sat beside the chair with his head on Brandts leg. "I need some advice Tallee. Thomaline's cats have all been what she considered pets. I guess they might have been bonded but we never realized this was a possibility and they have always been with the two of us. I don't know how this pairing arrangement really works."

"Thomaline should be able to help you with this. She has worked here with the soldiers and yaral that make up the Queen's Brigade."

"I'd like to learn from you if you don't mind. Alred is quirky enough, but I have a feeling that this one could be worse. He acts differently and I don't know why."

As Tallee thought about the problem, Thrad stood with his front paws on Brandt's leg and yowled before dropping to the floor and walking towards the door. There, he sat and looked back at Brandt and then scratched lightly on the wood.

"I think he wants to leave." Tallee observed.

"Yes, but where to? And how do you housebreak a cat of this age? The fortress servants will run away if they have deal with that!"

Tallee laughed again. "I do not believe that will be a problem. I can help you train with him, but it would probably be best just to spend as much time with him as you can. You can both learn each other's ways and when he is older you can always train here, either just with me or with the Brigade."

"I guess I'll decide when I find out how we get along together. You keep saying that he is young but just how old is he? He's not much smaller than the other cats that are here."

"What is his name?"

"It's Thrad. Why?"

"I'll try calling him. Thrad! Come here." Tallee also gestured for the cat to come away from the door. Thrad looked at Brandt and then back at the door.

"You try, please."

"Thrad. Come away from the door." Brandt commanded, sounding stern. Tallee smirked when Thrad just gave an angry swish of his tail.

"Do not command, just ask." Tallee suggested.

Brandt rolled his eyes, but did as Tallee suggested. The cat looked to be considering the request before he left the door and slowly walked back to Brandt.

"I want to show you some things." Tallee then pointed out why he thought Thrad was much younger than the usual yaral that came to Goldenspire. When the lesson was over he said, "You will see him develop quite quickly from now on. He must have been a late kitten. This might be a good thing as the bond between the two of you should be even stronger."

"Thank you. We'll leave you now as I have a lot to think about. I never expected anything like this, and I shudder to think of what Alred will show him. I can't image life here if they are anything alike!"

Tallee thought the next few months would be very interesting as he closed his door behind the most unlikely pair.

Brandt was just entering the courtyard when a cry rang out from one of the gate sentries.

"Riders! Riders My Lord." The guard called when he saw Brandt.

"Who?" Brandt cried as he rushed to the main door. He had come away with no weapons!

More soldiers had joined the guard, and all were straining to see in the darkness. Brandt could just faintly hear the sounds of racing horses. The noise was getting louder as they approached.

"It is General Temor!" Cried one of the soldiers.

"Wait! Be sure before you open the gate." Brandt demanded. He wanted no imposters gaining entrance.

"It is. I recognize him and his guard." The soldier stated and then he called down so that the gate was opened for the returning General.

After the party had thundered through the gate, Temor spotted Brandt on the steps. Hurriedly he dismounted from his horse and then Temor rushed up the steps.

"We have a problem, My Lord."

CHAPTER THIRTEEN

Looking past Temor's shoulder, Brandt could see that several of the soldiers were injured and had to be helped from their horses.

"What happened?" Brandt looked into the strained face of the general.

"Where is the Queen?" Temor countered. "She needs to hear this as well."

Before Brandt could answer or ask more questions, Skith came through the now open doors along with more guards. As he took in the scene before him, Skith called out for someone to send for healers and told Brandt and Temor to follow him. Once inside they were soon met by Thomaline.

"Temor! Are you injured?" She asked as she rushed to the general.

"No. Not me, but several of my soldiers were hurt. We need to speak privately My Lady."

"Come to our rooms."

Thomaline led the way, but they were joined by Leonde as they passed her doorway.

"What has happened? Why this uproar?"

"Come with us and Temor will explain."

Once they were all ensconced in the royal suite, Brandt passed around wine to all as they sat at the table.

"I told Brandt that we have a problem, but that should have been problems." Temor paused to take a long draught of the wine.

"Tell me." Thomaline directed while Alred settled by her side and Thrad sat near Brandt. Leonde looked appraisingly at all four.

"Firstly, when we arrived at the border outpost there was only one of the two guards we were searching for on their roster. The guard that went by the name of Ruthor never arrived there. The guard that was there, is named Neddel. He claims that their contingent was stopped before they arrived at the outpost.

There had been a message for Ruthor that stated he was needed elsewhere. The leader of that squad of soldiers insisted that you signed the order My Queen. Ruthor left for his new assignment, and no one has seen him since he rode away."

"When was this? How long has he been gone?" Thomaline asked.

"They were sent to relieve that outpost more than two months ago."

"What does anyone know about this Ruthor?" Brandt asked.

"It seems to be the familiar pattern." Temor told them. "No one knows much about him. He is quiet, does his job and keeps to himself."

"And disappears!" Thomaline clenched her fists. "It is probably the same elf. This Ruthor and this Moroth could be one and the same."

"I would hope so," Brandt muttered, "I don't want to even think that there is more than one imposter running around Goldenfell."

"Oh, but there is!" Exclaimed Leonde, "Do not forget that Mendeth has the same capability. We do not know the extent of his ability but there are at least two of them."

"Yes," agreed Temor, "and we do not know which one is which."

"I think I may have an idea." Skith said. "Mendeth was no soldier. Not in the whole time that he was here in Goldenspire. He despised soldiers and I never saw him take part in physical exercise. I would think that impersonating any soldier would be beyond and beneath him."

"If that is true, then the other is a very busy elf." Leonde stated.

"Were there any problems at the border? What did the commander have to report?" asked Thomaline.

"Nothing out of the ordinary. Their patrol was quiet with nothing remarkable observed either on our side or the other." Temor reported.

"Then what are the other problems you mentioned." Leonde asked. It was getting late.

"You did not see when we rode in My Lady, but we were attacked! Several of my guard were injured although thankfully, no one was killed. At least not among my soldiers."

"Explain! Where and when did this happen?" Thomaline commanded the general

"It was a day and a half ago. Just as we started out on the trail to Goldenspire. We were ambushed by assailants hidden in the brush along the trail. We never expected that kind of threat! We were close to Goldenspire and as far as we knew, we had no enemies!"

"How many were there? Could you tell?" Brandt asked. Temor had been accompanied by a group of twenty. It would have taken a large group to attack well-armed soldiers, even from ambush.

"It is difficult say. We were hardly in battle formation, but I do believe that I was their target. The main thrust of the attack was against me. Firstly, it was arrows and then when a few of my soldiers were wounded, attackers came from the brush at me. It was a hard fight before we could flee. I would guess that there were at least a dozen, maybe more. We had to run through another barrage of arrows a few miles later on but after that there were no more attackers. We have ridden as hard as we could since then."

"This could have been the work of Prince Cathos," Thomaline speculated, "but we can do nothing more tonight. Temor, see to your soldiers. Have more guards posted along the walls tonight and tomorrow we will meet here after breakfast. I have some thoughts about what might be happening, but I cannot be too hasty."

Everyone agreed and Temor was anxious to see those who had been wounded. If it had not been for them, he might not have been there to make a report.

Before Brandt bolted the door to their rooms, he heard Skith issue an order for the guards to be doubled by their chambers and also at the entrance to the corridor before that. This would help to ensure the safety of Leonde as well.

"What do you think?" He asked Thomaline as they both got ready for bed.

"I still think that Prince Cathos is behind this somehow. Probably Mendeth and his accomplice as well."

"But to what end? If Cathos planned to move against you, he would never succeed. Goldenfell would never follow that idiot's rule!"

"I believe as you do Brandt but who knows what Cathos believes."

As Brandt climbed into bed, he began to turn over scenarios in his mind. Sleep would be a long time coming.

When Thomaline had settled on her side of the bed, Alred suddenly jumped up, ready to take his spot as well. Thrad did not want to be left out and stood, paws on the bed, searching for a space to call his own.

"Oh No! Not you too." Brandt said harshly to his new companion. "Thomaline, this can't be allowed!"

"I agree. It is getting too crowded in here. Alred! Get down!"

Alred did not want to get down and Thrad just stood watching.

"Alred! Down!" Thomaline then gave the blankets a kick to get Alred's attention. "Down!"

Alred raised his head and stared at Thomaline. When she firmly repeated her command and pointed to the floor, Alred got up and with a grumbling rumble of a growl, finally did as he was told. Seeing that Alred was not going to be allowed to sleep on the bed, Thrad was then content to find a spot near the bedroom hearth while Alred settled on a place by the door.

"You know that we will pay for this, do you not?" Thomaline said to Brandt as they lay together in their bed.

"Maybe, but I'm hoping Alred's actions won't give Thrad any bad ideas."

"Thrad? Is that what you called him?"

"I just listed some names. That was the one he chose."

"Strange." Thomaline muttered and then she drifted off to sleep. Brandt stayed awake for hours.

The next morning, they rose early, and Brandt took Thrad out while Thomaline called for breakfast to be brought. Alred came along with them but when both cats hurried away leaving Brandt on his own, he returned to Thomaline. After a hasty meal they were soon greeting the others.

General Temor started by saying, "I sent out a squad of soldiers last night and I had Milron lead them. He is one of the best trackers we have, and I asked him to try and find our attackers. If they rode hard they should find the spot of the ambush later today."

"Good. We need evidence before I can point the blame at Cathos for being behind this assault." Said Thomaline.

"Why would he attack Temor?" Skith asked.

"I am sure he knows how such a loss would weaken me and in turn, all of Goldenfell and there is also the possibility that he tried to stop you reporting what you had learned from the border."

"I'd say it was the first fact you mentioned because Temor did not really learn much more than what we already guessed about our false guards and soldiers." Brandt said.

"Yes, but Cathos would not know that." Skith argued.

"I believe it was Cathos trying to weaken Thomaline's position. Without Temor, a military response might be weakened." Leonde stated.

"Thank you My Lady, but I am not that important. There was others that could take my place: Lord Brandt being chief among them." Temor highly regarded Brandt's expertise and thought that Cathos would dismiss the queen's consort's ability out of hand, to his own peril.

Brandt was heartened by the general's praise and confidence.

"Do we tell Princess Agretha?" Skith worried.

"No. I cannot believe that she would plot against me, but he is still her brother and who knows how he could use any knowledge she might possess." Thomaline did not want anyone to know what new threat might be waiting. "We must wait until Milron, and the others return. It would stir up too much trouble if we accuse Cathos without positive proof that can be shown to the Skellan Elves."

The meeting did not last long after that and all were cautioned about travelling or even going about their business alone.

"Leonde, I hope you will not be returning to your cottage." Thomaline pressed her grandmother for assurance.

"Do not concern yourself about me. I am staying here in Goldenspire, and I will help you in any way I can."

They were then interrupted by a yowl from the door. When Brandt opened it, Alred and Thrad strode in.

"Who is this?" Leonde questioned.

"Oh, I have not had time to tell you." Said Thomaline. "This is Thrad. He has decided that none of the soldiers that wish to become part of the Queen's Brigade would suit him and so he decided to attach himself to Brandt.

Leonde looked at Brandt and then back at the yaral until she broke out laughing.

"I'm glad you're amused. I didn't think it was funny." Brandt fumed but it was no use saying more as Leonde probably would not listen to his objections anyway.

"The only warning I have is for you Thomaline. Do not let your cat be a bad influence on this young one." That said, Leonde walked past the yaral, patting

Thrad on the head as she went by, and left the room. Thrad merely watched her go before he went to seek attention from Brandt.

"I am going to see the soldiers that were wounded. I might be able to help them."

"Be careful! Leonde warned me not to let you do too much healing unless she was there. Maybe you should ask her to accompany you."

"I will do that. What will you do?"

"I'm going to see Master Greth and then I'm going to the forge. If you need me, send word."

Brandt wanted to get in a workout with his sword but did not want to be debilitated by a session with Master Broday. He also wanted to finish the sword he was working on with the armorer. He had high hopes for that weapon.

Thomaline caught up with her grandmother before she had made it to her rooms. Leonde readily agreed to accompany Thomaline to the infirmary as she was anxious to see the healing ability firsthand and she also wanted to make sure that Thomaline did no harm to herself.

When they entered the infirmary, she saw that there were five wounded laying on cots. Only one seemed to be seriously injured.

"My Queen! How may we assist?" The healer asked when they entered.

"It is how I may assist you. I have the ability to heal, and I thought to help as you direct."

The healer was flattered by the offer but did not know how much good his Queen could manage.

"If you would like, there are some minor hurts that need attention." He said and directed Thomaline to the three least hurt among the soldiers. These had been deemed too minor for assisted healing and left to mend in the traditional manner.

"Shall I send for one of your guards?" Leonde asked Thomaline.

"I suppose we should. Ask for Ilan. I have the best results with him, but I will not need him for these three." The soldiers did not have serious wounds and before Leonde returned from sending a messenger for Ilan, Thomaline had healed them.

"Do not tell anyone about this. I am not ready to reveal the extent of my ability." She admonished both the soldiers and the astonished healer.

"My Queen! That was amazing! None of us can do that so easily!" The healer gushed to Thomaline.

"That is why you must not disclose what I have done. I cannot heal everyone!" She saw that Ilan had come as summoned and now she went over to the two more seriously wounded soldiers. She did not need the healer to tell her that one was near death. The healer had done what he could but that had been far from enough.

"Ilan, will you assist me? Be warned that this carries risk because I have never tried this kind of healing before."

"My Queen, I trust that you will not hurt me. You must try." Ilan knew the wounded elf.

"Thomaline, you need to take your time with this. You cannot just instinctively use your healing ability here. You must think your way through the process before you start and as you go, or you might do more harm than good." Leonde could easily see how this more elaborate healing could seriously affect Ilan and Thomaline.

Taking Leonde's warning seriously, Thomaline sat beside the wounded soldier and began by trying to sense where he was hurt and how badly. She had to know what needed to be repaired. Slowly, a picture began to develop in her mind and a course of actions became clearer.

"Ilan, come here please."

Ilan stood beside the cot and Thomaline took his hand when offered. Next she placed her other hand above the most serious of the soldier's wounds.

"Get ready Ilan and if you must, break contact with me. I do not want to hurt you."

The healer brought up a stool and Thomaline told Ilan to sit. When he had done so, she began to heal the soldier's wound. When she was finished, the healer moved to quickly examine were the arrow wound had been.

"It's gone! There is barely a scar now!"

Leonde was not interested in the wound, she wanted to know how Thomaline was feeling.

"I am fine. Ilan? What about you?"

"I feel a bit lightheaded but that is all."

"That is all for you today Ilan. You may go if you feel that you can stand. Can you send word to Staf for me. I will need her for the next wound."

Ilan seemed to walk off with no major ill effect and Thomaline waited for the next guard to appear. The soldier on the cot had one more wound and she knew that if she could repair that, he would recover. While she waited, Thomaline went to the last soldier to see what she would need to do for him.

"I will need another volunteer to heal this one." She told Leonde. "He is not too badly wounded but I cannot treat the others and not him."

When Staf appeared, Thomaline quickly explained what was happening and then went to the most badly wounded soldier where she was able to use her ability once more. Staf felt the effect more than Ilan, but she too was able to leave under her own power. After she had waited for a while and no other guard or soldier appeared, the Healer presented himself to help her heal the last elf.

"Please, I wish to see how this is done. Use me, My Queen." He requested.

"You might get more out of the experience than you bargained for." She warned but the healer did not back away. When the last soldier was healed of his wound, the healer was in need of a cot himself. His essence did not work well with Thomaline's power.

CHAPTER FOURTEEN

Thomaline was thankful that word of her healing power had not leaked out. Even though she had warned the soldiers and the healer not to speak of it, she was gratified to know that they had kept their word. That seemed to be the only good news. The patrol that Temor had sent in search of his assailants had not yet returned and there had been no word regarding the whereabouts of Prince Cathos. Despite this worry, Princess Agretha had sent a message to some of the outer settlements around Goldenspire, asking for volunteers from among the Skellan, to come with her and assist in the building of their new home. As her people had more soldiers than craftsmen, she asked for their help first. Agretha had finally settled upon the name of Pellisgould which meant "new hope" in the old Skellan language.

"Have you had any news?" Agretha asked Thomaline as she approached her in the courtyard. "I heard riders earlier."

"I was just coming to fetch you. Two of your messengers have returned and need to speak with you." Thomaline told the princess. "They are at the stables. Do you want me to send for them?"

"No. I will go and talk to them." Agretha did not have much else to occupy her time at the moment but when her volunteers arrived, they would start for the new colony within a day or so.

Thomaline bade her goodbye and went in search of Brandt. He was supposed to be working with the armorer, and she was eager to see the sword that he said would be finished that day. Unfortunately, she did not have a chance to get there before a shout from the gate caught her attention. The patrol was back!

General Temor joined her as she went to speak with the patrol commander. "Do you have news?" she asked.

"Nothing good I am afraid to say, My Queen." The commander nodded to the general before turning back to speak with Thomaline. "We found the trail easily enough. Three of the enemy had been wounded. We tracked them for two days before the trail split. One at a time, they began to take different routes until those tracks disappeared as well. We looked for days but found nothing. Whoever they are, they are very skilled in the woods." The commander did not like to make excuses but that was all he could offer.

"Could you tell who they were? Were they from Goldenfell or Skellan?"

"I could not answer that My Queen. They left nothing behind that would identify them. I am sorry."

"Do not be sorry. Your news is a disappointment but that is hardly your fault." Thomaline turned away while Temor spent time further questioning everyone in the patrol.

"Nothing!" His anger was apparent. "We are no further ahead!" He said when he rejoined her.

"But it is not surprising, is it? Although we all agree that Cathos is involved I did not think that he would tip his hand this soon. He is still plotting."

Muttering dire consequences upon the prince, Temor walked with Thomaline into the fortress hall. Her thoughts of joining Brandt at the forge had been forgotten.

Unaware that Thomaline had thought to join him, Brandt was putting the finishing touches on his new sword. The armorer had finally given it his approval and it was just the sword handle that needed to be fitted to Brandt's grip. He was very proud of his work.

"I want to see what the Queen thinks. I'd like to make her one next." He told his tutor.

"The Queen already has a good sword that has served her well over the centuries, but I am sure that she would welcome a weapon such as yours, My Lord, especially as you would be the maker. It is excellent work." The armorer could offer no higher praise and Brandt beamed with pleasure. Another hour or so and he would be able to show off his skill.

Tallee was also hard at work, but he did not have anything to show off! Thomaline and Brandt had sent their yaral to Tallee that morning after asking him to start training the younger cat in some of the basics commands used by the soldiers of the Queen's Brigade. Alred was sent along with Thrad as he was still unsure of himself unless he was in the company of the other cat or Brandt himself. Tallee was nearing the stage of giving up in despair. The yaral was clearly uninterested and totally uncooperative and Alred was no help at all!

When Brandt left the forge area with his new sword, he stopped at the cat barracks to collect Thrad. Tallee was sitting on a bench while the two cats wrestled on the floor.

"How did your training session go?" Brandt asked before he noticed how despondent Tallee looked.

"It did not, My Lord! He totally ignores me. It is as if I do not exist." Tallee had never had a problem like this. Not with any of the many animals he had dealt with.

"It's probably all Alred's fault." Said Brandt.

"No, My Lord. I do not believe that is the problem this time, but I do not know what is."

Trying to break up the mock fight before them, Brandt called to Thrad. He had to call three times, but eventually Thrad joined him and proceeded to rub hard against Brandt's legs.

"I think he is just too young." Stated Tallee. "He seems to listen well enough to you, but he is not interested in anyone else." Then Tallee had a thought. "The issue could be the trauma he suffered from attack. He never goes anywhere alone. Maybe he does not trust anyone but you and the Queen." Tallee reason.

"You could be right. Neither Thomaline nor I have had any unusual issues." Although with the yaral there were always minor problems. "I just thought that he might benefit from your guidance when I don't have enough time."

"Then I suggest that you tell him that, My Lord. He might do as you ask."

Brandt had to consider that idea and promised Tallee he would try but his attention was diverted as a messenger was coming through the gate with news for the Queen.

"What is it?" he asked when he approached the elf.

"My Lord. I should wait for the Queen or General Temor."

"Tell me and I will go and find them." Brandt could see that the messenger was struggling with the decision. His instructions had been to find the Queen. Would he be derelict in his duty if he gave the news to the Consort?

The decision was made for him when he heard a shout from across the courtyard. The Queen was on her way.

"What is it?" Thomaline asked when both she and Temor joined Brandt and the waiting messenger.

"It is bad news My Queen! There has been an attack on the village of Woldenfell!"

Woldenfell was farther down the mountain, on the other side of her old home of Goldenhollow and that was days from Goldenspire.

"Details! Now!" Commanded General Temor. Now was no time for dramatics.

"The village was struck by over twenty armed bandits. Three of the villagers were killed and five more were injured. The bandits took all the food that they could carry!" The messenger reported.

"Bandits? I do not believe it! Where have bandits sprung from?" Temor was incensed at the idea. This was Goldenfell! They had never had bandits!

"I do not believe it was bandits." Said Thomaline as she looked grimly at Brandt. "Someone else we know is in need of supplies."

Temor understood to whom she was referring and turned to call up to the sentries above the fortress gates. "Send me your commander! Then shut and bar the gates. No one is to enter or leave without your commander's permission."

Brandt and Thrad followed Thomaline and Temor as they hurried into the fortress. He just knew that this would necessitate the need for another meeting! He was correct.

Thomaline called for Skith and the rest of the council to attend an emergency session while she went in search of Leonde. She did not get far before she was stopped by Princess Agretha. The princess looked equally worried.

"I must speak with you. It is urgent." Agretha told Thomaline. "I have information that you need to hear."

Thomaline was about to brush off the princess's request while she dealt with this new crisis, but Agretha would not be gainsaid.

"It is to do with Cathos!" Agretha declared and Thomaline could see that it was indeed important.

"All right. I will find Leonde and then you must come to the council chambers and meet with the rest of us."

"I will go there now."

Brandt and his four-legged shadow went to join the others. Along the way, Alred joined them. Soon everyone was seated in the council chamber.

"We have been informed that an attack has occurred on the village of Woldenfell." Thomaline told the astonished gathering. "There have been casualties, but the main thrust of the raid seems to have been for supplies." There were angry voices around the table until Thomaline continued. "The messenger said it was bandits. We know that we have never had bandits!"

"Do you know who has done this?" Skith asked.

"I am afraid that I do." Agretha answered and there was a hush around the table as most of the councilors stared at her in suspicion. "Before your messenger arrived, I received messages of my own. I had sent word to settlements where many of my own soldiers were living, asking for volunteers to travel to the site of our new home and help with the construction. What I have just learned is that many of those soldiers are missing."

The council room erupted in angry shouts and hurled accusations.

"Quiet!" Shouted Skith, before Thomaline could enter into the fray. The loud voices stopped but the angry looks did not. "Go on Agretha."

"I had only contacted a few settlements as I had thought to send for workers in rotation but with the exception of two of the villages, many of the soldiers among my people have gone. I have been told that they left singly or in very small groups and did not draw attention to their actions. They have been slipping away for days. I have sent messengers back to tell some of those that remain to come here and report to me. I must know what is happening."

"I think I can tell you." Said Brandt. "They have been slipping off to join your brother. It was not bandits that attacked Woldenfell, it was Prince Cathos! He is gathering soldiers and now they need supplies."

Princess Agretha appeared to pale at that statement and Skith started to turn to Brandt, planning on admonishing him for upsetting the princess but Agretha spoke before that could happen.

"I believe Lord Brandt may be correct. As you know, Cathos has been missing for days as well and I have had no word from him. I hate to say this, but he could have been planning some action for a long time. From what I have just learned, our soldiers had been disappearing for days even before Cathos left."

"Temor, start calling up our soldiers. I want a staging area set up for when they arrive. We have a larger force than Prince Cathos so at the moment I do not know what he hopes to achieve, but I want our people ready."

"What about the villages and other settlements? We need protection for them as well. Crops have been planted and herds need tending." Skith reminded Thomaline.

"All that could factor into Cathos's plans." Brandt added. "He knows that with attacks on vulnerable villages he can get all the supplies he wants. He must also know that you will send troops to protect them. That will lessen the number of soldiers that you can call to Goldenspire to fight against him if it comes to that. If you try to protect all your scattered people, the number of soldiers that you will command with be almost the same as his."

"You will have more than my brother. As I said, my messengers say that not all our soldiers have gone over to him. I must believe that more will remain loyal to me, and I will give you what assistance I may."

Thomaline remained silent as she considered everything she had just heard. As much as she would like to trust the princess, Thomaline knew that for now at least, Agretha would not be privy to any more of their decisions. It was an action that would lay heavily for Thomaline as she now considered the princess to be a friend and had been happy with the way their relationship had progressed.

"Thank you Agretha. Your offer is appreciated but for now I cannot accept it. You need to learn the full extent of the betrayal committed by your brother. When you have learned all that you can and know who is still loyal to you, then we will speak again but for now I must deal with this new threat to Goldenfell. I am afraid that there is much more to the machinations of Cathos."

Agretha understood but it was with a sorrowful heart that she left the council chamber. Cathos was setting out to ruin the best things that had ever happened to Agretha, and she silently vowed that she would do everything she could to stop him and help Thomaline!

Skith had said nothing as he watched the princess leave the room. His sadness was carefully hidden but Thomaline and Brandt understood the depth of his emotions no matter how carefully he kept his demeanor benign.

"Temor, have someone keep eyes on the princess. I want to know who she speaks with and if possible, what she does and instructs her messengers to do." Thomaline said.

"Despite your earlier words, do you believe that she is involved in a plot against you?" Skith's voice betrayed no feelings for the Skellan royal.

"I think that she is telling the truth as she knows it, but I cannot leave the safety of Goldenfell to my feelings alone. Cathos could involve her in ways she does not know. Do not forget that we have at least two with the ability to use their glamour to change their appearance. She might not even know who she is actually speaking with." Thomaline explained.

"That is a large problem." Temor spoke up. "How do any of us know if it is an imposter we speak with. It could be anyone."

"Temor is correct with his suspicions, but I think I can give you some assurance as to how these imposters go about their clandestine activities." Now it was Leonde's turn to speak up.

Thomaline was hopeful that her grandmother would offer them some insight that might give them an edge over Cathos and his plans. Alred had left his spot near the council doors and was now standing beside Thomaline. She was absently stoking the cat's head. Thrad had not left Brandt's side and had kept his head laid on Brandt's leg. Brandt had not yet contributed much to the conversation, but his mind was carefully turning over all that he was learning.

"What do you know?" Thomaline asked Leonde.

"I think you have all forgotten just how glamour works. You cannot change your appearance to look like someone else."

"But we have evidence of this!" Temor could hardly believe that Leonde could be so wrong.

"Do you? Think back. When Mendeth broke through our Ward using Thandel's talisman we thought he took on the appearance of Thandel, but he was not closely observed. Glamour does not let you become someone else, no matter how strong your ability may be. If your ability is strong enough, you can change your appearance to become more like the person you are trying to impersonate but based on your own body." Leonde waited while the group considered what she had said. "I did not know Thandel, but Mendeth must have had at least a passing resemblance to him to be able to fool the other scout."

"Temor, did he?" Thomaline asked her general. He had chosen the scouts and knew them best.

Temor thought carefully. Thandel had been one of the many soldiers under his command. "There were certain characteristics shared by the two. Height and build for a start."

"Yes, that would certainly be required. You cannot become taller, shorter, or even shed some weight. So, I think that Mendeth passed for Thandel because he was seen from a distance and from behind."

"What about someone posing as Dotha? How would he be able to fool the guards when they saw him? They knew Dotha. They would have had a good look at him." Brandt finally spoke up.

"I wonder if they did. Or were they fooled because they had no reason to doubt that they were seeing Dotha. It was also darker in that corridor. Would you have asked to see his face?"

"No. It was not the fault of the guards. You're right. We see what we expect to see." Brandt admitted. Dotha and the imposter must also have shared similarities.

"So, what do we do?" Skith asked as he looked around the room, firstly at his fellow councilors and then at Thomaline.

"We must be vigilant. We discuss nothing unless we are absolutely certain of who we are speaking with." Stated Thomaline although no one in the room was similar to Mendeth in size or shape. Unfortunately, they did not really know how the other impostor was built or if there was anyone else involved. So far there had not been any suggestion that a female was involved, and is would be almost impossible to pretend to be Leonde. There was something however, that was starting to niggle in her mind. It was something to do with glamour and who could use it!

Brandt felt his head start to hurt. This would lead to everyone second guessing what they were doing and with whom they were speaking. There would be no trust!

"Why not a code word of some kind?" He suggested.

"That is an excellent idea, Brandt." Said Thomaline. "Of course, we must try to clearly see who we are speaking with as well. I know from my own experience of using my small glamour ability that I can change the color of my hair and eyes, but I cannot change my face."

"Then this will be our code word." Skith stated and then he gave them the word.

"What is that? I don't understand." Brandt complained.

"It is an old word in an old Goldenfell dialect. The Skellan will not know it." Skith said. "I doubt that you will need to know what it means."

Brandt scowled and decided he would just ask Thomaline when they were alone.

"Then it is settled. The code is for those of us in this room." Thomaline directed.

Skith dismissed the council while the others remained.

"Thank you, Leonde. I had forgotten the limits of glamour in our wariness." Temor admitted.

"I am sorry that I did not think to mention it earlier. What are our plans now?" she asked Thomaline.

"As stated earlier. We call up our soldiers and make sure that we safeguard our outer villages. Even though I am certain this is part of what Cathos wants, we cannot leave our people undefended and open to more attacks. I will not, however, be drawn out in further conflict at this time. We need to prepare, and I want to give Agretha time to discover just how many of the Skellan remain loyal to her and how many have gone over to her brother."

At last! A message had been received. He would soon be allowed to go home!

CHAPTER FIFTEEN

More days passed. Soldiers had been summoned and vulnerable villagers had been brought closer to the fortress. Goldenspire was again home to refugees. Thomaline had previously thought that once their Ward had been replaced, this kind of danger would be a thing of the past! Where villagers once lived and worked their fields and tended their livestock, soldiers now patrolled. At least some of those could carry on the villagers' work and also help the ones that had stayed to protect their homes. This had lessened some of the concern that the soldiers Thomaline might need to counter whatever it was that Prince Cathos was planning, would be thinned too much by protecting outlying areas.

Left with nothing else to occupy her time, Princess Agretha had continued with her plans for her new home of Pellisgould. She had successfully called for the Skellan soldiers that had not run off to join her brother, to go to the new settlement and help with its construction. This had the added benefit of removing the soldiers from any influence of Cathos and his continued recruitment efforts. The numbers had been more than Agretha had expected. Messages had been received informing her of the construction progress and now it was time to lead another contingent of her people away from Goldenspire.

"You have been extremely generous with your supplies Thomaline, but I want to leave. My people will need me more than ever now that Cathos has abandoned them for his own purposes. The quicker we can build our new home, the faster the rest of the Skellan can move."

"I would like to see Pellisgould. I hope I can do so soon." Thomaline replied.

"And I will welcome you there. I will not, however, be welcoming my brother. I need to be quit of him. I can never forgive his abandonment of the

Skellan and myself in particular. He has given no thought to what I must be going through. For all he knows I could have been imprisoned or worse! That is why I must go now. I have plans of my own to see to."

Thomaline understood. "When will you go?"

"We are mostly ready now. I will send word for the wagons to be loaded today so that we can leave tomorrow morning."

"Very well. We will see you off, but I will miss you Agretha. It has almost been as if I had a sister."

"Thank you. I would gladly trade you for my brother." She laughed but was also serious. Cathos was now a total disgrace.

When Agretha left, Thomaline went to find Brandt. She wanted to speak with Skith, Temor and Leonde as well. Most meetings of the small group were now held in her private rooms.

"Well, Temor. Has there been any news from your scouts?" Thomaline asked.

"Some My Lady. Unfortunately, we have not found their main camp, but we have found evidence of smaller ones. They are still trying to raid some of the outer habitations but for the most part they have not been too successful. There have been a few injuries but no fatalities. Not on our part."

"Where do you think they might be hiding?" Skith asked.

"Not in the forests. My patrols have checked thoroughly. I must conclude that they are encamped on the plains somewhere."

"At least they're far from Goldenspire out there." Brandt observed.

"Yes, but that leads to other problems." Said the general. "Out there, even if we do find them, we would not be able to get close without being discovered. There is no cover, and I am sure that prince would choose the area for that reason."

"Why would Cathos be sitting out there? What does he hope to gain?" Not having a clear understanding of the princes' motives was aggravating for Thomaline. As was the waiting!

"When winter comes, he will find staying on the plains not the best place to be." Observed Skith.

"I doubt that he will be there for that season. I am sure that whatever plan Prince Cathos is hatching will be brought to fruition before then." Leonde stated.

"What of the border posts? Has there been any activity where the messages from the River Lord have been found?" Thomaline asked Temor.

"I think we should add more guards to that station." Brandt told them. "I can't help but believe that outpost has great importance to whatever it is that Cathos plans."

"Yes. They are tied together in whatever this is," agreed Skith, "Cathos, Mendeth and the River Lord."

When the others had left, Skith remained behind.

"What is it?" asked Thomaline.

"I ask that I might be allowed to go part way with Princess Agretha when she leaves in the morning." He said.

"Of course! You must make your own decisions regarding the princess. All that I ask is that you take precautions and have a suitable guard travel with you as you know what almost happened to Temor." Thomaline offered. "I cannot lose you and that is not just because you are the head of my council."

Skith bowed his head in acknowledgement and smiled. It had not been that many years ago that she would gladly have 'lost' him!

"I will be careful. Although if I possessed the ability of a strong glamour, a disguise would be helpful." He smiled again.

The comment broke open the dam on a memory for Thomaline! That was what had been lurking in the back of her mind for days.

"Skith! That is it!" She cried and then ran to the door and flung it open to the startlement of her guards. "Find General Temor! Tell him I need to speak with him urgently." She commanded.

"What My Lady? What have I said?" Skith asked as he tried to remember his previous words.

"Wait. I will tell you shortly."

Brandt had heard the commotion coming from their chambers and he returned just ahead of the general.

"Temor! You chose the scouts that were sent out with talismans two years ago. What do you know of the one sent south? The one who used his glamour to get the closest to one of their fortresses?"

Temor thought for a moment to remember which elf that was. "It was Morphas. It was he that got nearly into their camp."

"Yes, Morphas. But he more than got close to their fortress. If I remember correctly, he said that he was able to do so because of his strong glamour ability. Have we heard of anyone else that claimed to be able to do that?"

"No! Why did I not remember this? He never came forward to remind me when I had asked." Temor was clearly upset.

"Do you mean that he has been here in Goldenspire?" she asked.

"Yes! From time to time anyway. He has been at one of the outposts and when he has been here, I have used him as a scout." Temor told them.

"Then I believe we have found our chief spy." Thomaline claimed. "Was he at the outpost where the messages were found?"

"Yes My Lady, he was. But how could he be there and be Moroth at the same time?"

"I do not believe that he was. I think that he and Mendeth have been working together. Who knows which one was at the outpost? Maybe they both were there."

The speculation went on. They were now sure that Mendeth was in league with someone on the other side of the Ward barrier. The River Lord most probably. The real question was where Prince Cathos fit into the picture. Was he in a plot with Mendeth or was his treachery only for his own advancement? Even if he was working with Mendeth and the River Lord, what was in it for him?

Brandt was of the opinion that the two were working together but he was not sure about the River Lord's involvement. He knew that Cathos and Mendeth both would like to see him dead. Cathos wanted to replace him at the least, and upsurge Thomaline at the most. Mendeth had wanted him dead from the first day he arrived in Goldenspire, but he could not see him wanting to cause any harm to Thomaline even if he had tried to offer her to Cathos when those two had first met.

Thomaline was interrupted by a knock at the door. One of the guards came to tell her that she was needed in the courtyard. Someone was causing a disturbance by trying to gain entrance to the fortress.

As they all followed Thomaline, Leonde joined them and General Temor swiftly brought the former queen up to date. As they crossed the courtyard and approached the gate, shouts could be heard from the other side.

"Who is it?" Thomaline asked the gate warden.

"I do not know My Queen. She will not give her name."

Unnoticed by Thomaline, Leonde started to look slightly ill. It could not be, she thought.

Once again something was shouted from outside the gates.

"How many are out there?" Brandt asked.

"It is just one old woman and what looks like an equally old servant. There are no others My Lord." The gate warden said.

"Well, we cannot be afraid of one old woman." Thomaline said. "Let them in."

Leonde stiffened as the gate was opened and Brandt noticed a look of horror on her face when a goat cart bearing an incredibly old female elf followed by an equally old retainer hurried through the gates.

"It cannot be!" stated Leonde. "I thought she was dead!"

Brandt then heard her whisper. "At least I assumed she was!"

He thought this was going to be very interesting as he had never seen Thomaline's grandmother look so unsettled.

The goat cart was pulled to a stop in front of Thomaline.

"Who are you?" The driver querulously demanded. "Who is in charge here? What have you done with them?" The old elf looked around the courtyard.

Thomaline looked to Temor and Skith, but they wore the same look of confusion as she. What was going on?

"Well! Answer me!" was the next shouted demand.

Thomaline's mouth was open, but no words came quick enough for the old woman.

Brandt thought he heard Leonde whisper, "Why can she not be dead?"

Evidently that faint whisper was too loud as the elderly intruder got down and rounded the end of the cart with her servant's help and spied Leonde standing beside Brandt.

"Leonde! Is that you, you treacherous cow? I should have known!"

Leonde closed her eyes as if trying to banish the sight before her. Thomaline, Skith and Temor turned to look and Thomaline closed her mouth with a click.

"Who is this?" she asked her grandmother. Leonde did not have a chance to reply for the old woman turned to Thomaline and shouted once more.

"Who am I? Who am I? Who are you? I asked you before! Where are your manners girl?"

That was enough for Thomaline as her temper flared. Brandt took a step back and now stood behind Leonde. He did not think he wanted to be in the way of an explosion.

However, before Thomaline said something they would all regret, Skith stepped forward with diplomatic purpose.

"This is Thomaline; Queen of Goldenfell and your queen as well. Please, show respect." He said in a calming tone.

"Respect? Huh! Does she talk or just stand about gaping like fish?" The old one was not backing down and she kept shrugging off the hand of her servant. The servant looked ready to faint.

"Enough!" Thomaline shouted. "Who are you and what do you want?" Unfortunately, she was ignored.

"Is this your influence you worthless creature?" she addressed Leonde. "She must have gotten her manners from you." The woman gave a dismissive snort as she glared at Leonde before turning to look disdainfully at Thomaline. "I cannot think why he held you in any regard." She declared.

"Guards! Take this...this person and put her out the gate!" Thomaline demanded but as two moved forward to obey the order, Leonde finally found her voice.

"Wait. Wait Thomaline. Let her speak and then get rid of her."

"You would like that, would you not?" the other sneered.

"Yes I would. It would make me happy beyond belief!" Leonde fired back. "You are still under banishment after all!"

"Explain!" Thomaline's face was as red as sunset and Brandt thought she was about to explode!

"This," Leonde flung her arm towards the old woman, "is your grandfather's aunt. Her name is Bulgrid."

Thomaline looked in askance at Bulgrid. What a horrifying thought. "Aunt?" she asked, "Why have I never heard of you?"

Bulgrid ignored the question and instead looked daggers at Leonde.

It was Leonde that replied. "That is because my husband had me banish her! That was so long ago I thought that surely she must have died by now!"

Leonde was now angry. Everyone else was dead. Why could not Bulgrid have managed to do the same!

"What do you want Bulgrid? Who are you looking for?" Thomaline asked.

"I want my grandsons. I have not heard from them in quite a while. They always came to visit, and they have not done so. What have you done with them?"

"Who are they and why should I have done something to them?" Thomaline looked at Bulgrid and then Leonde.

"I do not know. I did not know she had any." Leonde answered, her late husband Gendith had had one cousin: Bulgrid's son. When she had banished her husband's aunt, Bulgrid's son had gone with his mother and that was the last Leonde had ever heard of either of them; until now.

"I want to sit down." Bulgrid suddenly declared.

"Sit on your cart!" Leonde was the opposite of gracious.

"I do not know who your grandsons are." Thomaline tried again. "What are their names?"

"As if you do not know! You know one very well!"

Brandt was starting to wonder if Bulgrid was just stubborn or so old that she was losing her mind. Did that happen to elves? It was another thing he would have to ask Palin whenever they finally had time for that frank discussion he had kept postponing.

It was Skith's turn to try. "Bulgrid, no one has told us that you were their grandmother. What are the names of your grandsons, and we will try to find them." He said as kindly as he could.

"Do not speak to me in that tone! You know very well who I am talking about! He worked with you long enough!"

Why would she not give them a name!

Skith tried once more, "Who?"

"Mendeth, you fool!" shouted Bulgrid. "Where is Mendeth!"

Brandt could hardly believe what she had said, although if made perfect sense after meeting Bulgrid. He certainly knew where Mendeth had come by his sparkling personality!

"Your grandson is Mendeth? Well then, who is the other one?" General Temor asked before realizing that now he too would be drawn into this farce.

"Who are you?" she asked suspiciously.

"I am General Temor. Please, what is the name of your other grandson?"

"It is Morphas! Have you lost him too?" Bulgrid sneered as she crossed her arms over her chest.

Yes. Just like Mendeth, Brandt thought.

"We definitely need to talk." Said Thomaline. "Come into the fortress and I will explain."

"Not if she is going to be there!" Bulgrid pointed to Leonde.

"Yes, you will too, and my grandmother will certainly be there. You have come to me for answers and now you will obey your Queen! If you need assistance, I am sure one of the guards can help you to our hall." Thomaline was done with this conversation. Once they were inside, there would be another.

Before Thomaline could call for the assistance of a guard, Bulgrid's aggrieved servant came forward to offer his mistress his arm and after a whispered word in her ear, they started to follow Skith as he led the way.

"I know where I am going!" She said loudly to his back. "I have been here before you know!"

"Can this day get any worse?" said Thomaline as she and Leonde started to follow them, with Brandt bringing up the rear.

She should never have asked as before they made it to the steps there was a terrified bleat and then the goat cart went tearing across the courtyard chased by two yaral. Alred had led Thrad into finding entertainment as they had become bored with all the shouting!

CHAPTER SIXTEEN

Brandt was laughing so hard that he had scant breath left to call to Thrad away from his chase. Thomaline was angry and the look she sent his way should have sobered him on the spot, but he was still bent over with laughter. Agretha and some of her people were near her wagons as they had been giving instructions to the workers and now they stood, gaping at the sight. Tallee was quicker to act, however, and he rushed forward and was able to grab a rein of one of the two huge goats that drew Bulgrid's cart. As he hung on, trying to stop the beasts, he at least was able to shout for Alred and Thrad to stop their chase, as well as hurling several insults their way.

Thomaline was furious with everyone! First this abusive old woman and now the yaral! Brandt should have tried to deal with the situation, but he was useless as he stood there, his shoulders still shaking as he wiped the tears of laughter from his eyes. As she watched his continuing mirth, she finally started to relax and when he looked directly at her, she began to smile. Soon she was laughing as well at the ridiculous situation and then the others joined her. The exception was, of course, Bulgrid.

Bulgrid was not amused. Brandt thought that she had probably never been amused in her entire long life.

"You! You are the one!" Bulgrid had turned to see who was laughing and for the first time, paid attention to his presence. "You are that abomination!"

Brandt soon got himself under control and addressed her comment.

"Yes, I am Brandt, the Queen's Consort. I'm glad to see that you've heard of me." He gave a small bow, and his reply was insolent, but he could not see why he should try and appease someone like Bulgrid. He had never had any success in that endeavor with Mendeth and he was not going to waste his breath with Bulgrid.

It appeared that Bulgrid was so incensed that she could not manage further speech as her mouth merely opened and closed soundlessly.

Thomaline and Leonde alike were glad to see that someone could shut the old harridan up.

Now that they could see that Tallee had the goats firmly in hand and that the yaral had quit their game, Thomaline called to Alred and the cat came to her, followed by his younger shadow. The Skellan stood by their wagons still looking shocked by the recent activity.

"Tallee, would you please take care of those animals, but keep them ready. Their owner will not be here long." Thomaline called and then ignored the huff of protest she heard from Bulgrid. "Come along everyone. We meet in the Council rooms." She instructed.

Brandt continued to follow the rest of their little group as he gestured for Thrad to join him. When the cat had fallen into step by his side, he said, "Was that fun?"

Thrad look up at him and if a cat could smile, Thrad did.

"I'm glad you enjoyed that because I don't want to see you do something like that again." Brandt kept his voice low, but stern. "You embarrassed Thomaline, and I will not have that." He did not know if Thrad understood his words or just his tone, but the yaral did not look quite so happy now. They were the last to enter the Council chamber.

Brandt quickly took his place beside Thomaline, and the others settled in to learn what they could from Bulgrid.

Thomaline had requested that a servant attend them, and wine and water were served to the group. Bulgrid downed her wine in two gulps and held out her goblet for more.

"Leave her the wine." Leonde instructed. She knew that Bulgrid would only keep asking for more anyway.

"Enough! I am here. Tell me where my grandsons are."

"We do not know." Thomaline started to explain but before she could, Bulgrid tried to butt in.

From long experience with her late husband's aunt, Leonde forestalled the next tirade. "Bulgrid, Mendeth left Goldenspire two years ago. We do not know when exactly Morphas disappeared, but he did so willingly and is probably with Mendeth."

Bulgrid gulped another goblet of wine and then asked, "Why did Mendeth leave? He told me that he had an important mission to accomplish for the Queen and that he might not see me for a while. He was on a mission that concerned that one!" she pointed a gnarled finger at Brandt.

"When was this?" Skith asked although he was sure he knew the answer.

"Two years ago. He came to gather some of his belongings and left. He said his mission was urgent!"

Now they knew where he had initially disappeared to when he had been dismissed.

"What about Morphas? When was the last time you saw him?" Skith again asked the question.

"Last winter. He told me that he would be too busy to visit me as he was working on a vital plan that involved all of Goldenfell. I knew that he was important to the kingdom and accepted what he said, but there has been no further word from him. Now what have you done with them?"

As Skith's diplomacy seemed to be keeping Bulgrid as calm as she was likely to get, he continued his discussion with her. "I do not know what stories you have heard from your grandsons, but I will to tell you the truth. Mendeth was dismissed from the Queen's Council two years ago." Skith got no further before Bulgrid erupted in anger.

"Why? Mendeth told me that he was your closest ally. I do not believe that! How could you dismiss him?"

"Please, calm yourself and let me explain." Skith patiently said.

Leonde thought that he was wasting his breath. Her old antagonist would hear only what she wanted to hear, no matter what he told her.

Skith then laid out for Bulgrid exactly what had happened, before, during and after that Xarlerii threat had been dealt with. He also tried to explain Mendeth's treachery and the murder he had committed, but Bulgrid would hear nothing negative about her grandson. It was pointless to even try to explain about Morphas!

Thomaline broke through the old woman's ranting. "Whether you believe Skith or not, Mendeth and Morphas are traitors to Goldenfell, but at this time we do not know their whereabouts. Go home Bulgrid. We cannot help you now. If you tell us where you live, I will send word to you when we find your grandsons."

"I believe nothing you say. You are an upstart, and you are a fool if you are guided by that one!" Bulgrid snarled at Thomaline as she pointed to Leonde. Leonde merely sighed and hoped this would all be over soon. "As for the disgrace that sits beside you; Mendeth was correct. He should have been eliminated as soon as you brought him to Goldenfell! I will rejoice the day when he is gone and someone worthy sits beside you or even in your place!" she spat.

Thomaline was not going to listen to anymore. She called for a guard and instructed him to take Bulgrid and her servant to their goat cart and to see them from the fortress. Bulgrid would not be granted access to Goldenspire in the future as her banishment would be enforced.

"Now that she is gone Leonde, would you please explain for what that was all about?" Thomaline was tired from all the yelling and ranting and she was hoping that Leonde would unravel the mystery that was Bulgrid.

"If I must." Leonde began and then she took a drink from her previously untouched wine. "My husband Gendith was a prince of this land as was his father, but Bulgrid had no title. Gendith's aunt has always been jealous of that fact and that her nephew married the Queen while her own son was far less connected to the ruling of Goldenfell. She did, however, reside in this fortress after we were married. Her husband had died quite young and Gendith felt some responsibility for her and her young son. His cousin was not an ambition person. Malpith's interests lay in beauty and art, and he was an amazing sculptor. Many of his works still adorn rooms in this fortress. Bulgrid's ambition knew no boundaries however for she possesses none. Constantly she was at Gendith to use his marriage to me to enrich her and increase her standing in the kingdom to that as she thought she deserved. We had to endure so many years with her until one day Gendith reached his limits of family duty and patience. He never did tell me just what she had done that finally caused him to act, but he told me that she must go and that if I did not banish her, he would leave! Thomaline, you never knew me before you came back to Goldenfell and Gendith died before your father came of age. I believed that Gendith would do exactly as he said and so I did as he demanded. Bulgrid was banished but somehow, she made her son go with her. That was an unseen wrinkle as your grandfather was very fond of his cousin. I do not know where they eventually settled and until today, I have not seen her for all these long years. I truly had thought she would have died and had forgotten about her."

This was an incredibly long speech for Leonde, and it still did not explain as much as Thomaline wanted but Leonde was not finished.

"When Bulgrid and her son left Goldenspire, he was not married, and I do not know whom he did wed. She must have been someone from where they made a new home."

"I wonder where that was. Mendeth never talked about his family." Skith offered.

"Somewhere remote I would think." Temor broke into the narrative. "This has all the elements of something very secretive."

"It is more than that." Leonde stated. "It raises a huge problem that I had never foreseen."

Thomaline looked at Brandt and found that his frown was as grim as hers. "What now?"

"You are the last of my royal line Thomaline and only you share that blood. However, there is also mingled in your heritage, that of Gendith. This makes Mendeth and Morphas distant cousins to you as the three of you share Gendith's father's bloodline." She was met with baffled looks from the others. "When I created the new Ward, I made it in tune with our blood. We were the only two that could make any changes. Now however, I have been presented with a fact that will alter that knowledge. Thomaline can control the Ward and as Mendeth and Morphas share blood with her, they too will have some affinity with it. Leyrd made the previous Ward and Mendeth's affinity with it would have been strong. When Mendeth went and found the Skellan we thought that he used the talisman to get through the boundary. I now believe that his escape was more to do with his being able to manipulate the Ward than it was the use of the talisman. He will be able to something similar with the current Ward."

The others looked at Leonde with dawning horror! Mendeth previously had proven that he was a danger to all of Goldenfell. What damage was he planning to cause now?

"I know that one of his goals is to eliminate me." Brandt stated. "After that I think he'll look for a replacement consort."

"He already has one in mind." Thomaline said. "He must have been planning this ever since we had him arrested when the Skellan first joined us."

"Do we tell Princess Agretha?" Skith asked.

"No!" said Thomaline sharply. "She leaves as planned. I do not doubt her motives but her going to Pellisgould takes many of her people and especially her soldiers with her. The more she can draw away, the less the prince can call to his banner."

"We may still have some divided loyalties." Temor pointed out. "Some of our people were going to go there and quite a few of hers were staying here."

"Our people can still go, but not any of the soldiers. We will need them now." Thomaline tried to think what to do.

Brandt thought that Mendeth and his brother posed the most immediate threat. "If Mendeth plans to bring re-enforcements from outside of Goldenfell to join with the prince we must deal with him first. If Cathos is contained here, he can be isolated and dealt with later."

"Brandt is correct. Mendeth must have a plan in place to get aide from beyond our borders." Temor agreed.

"But for whom is the aide?" Leonde asked. "I must admit that I am struggling to understand why he would be in league with this River Lord."

"I do not think anything about this plan, or plans is straightforward. Mendeth always seemed to think around corners. We do not know if Cathos and Mendeth plot together or if Mendeth plots with the River Lord." Thomaline's mind was swirling with possibilities. "Say nothing to Agretha and we will see her and her fellow travelers off tomorrow. Once they have gone, we will address what we have learned today."

When they had all gone their separate ways, Brandt went down to the main courtyard. His reasons were two-fold. He wanted to ensure that Bulgrid had been safely escorted from the fortress and he wanted to see Tallee. He found him in his usual place in the barracks.

"That was some excitement, My Lord." Tallee said when Brandt found him.

"I know! Thankfully, you were able to grab that goat team. I'm afraid I was completely useless. I don't think I've laughed so much since I got here."

"I have never seen a goat harnessed before. Where did that awful woman come from?"

"That awful woman is the aunt of the Queen's grandfather." Brandt explained and Tallee was instantly chagrined. "Don't worry Tallee. We all thought she was a horror. Especially Leonde." Brandt chuckled at the thought.

The whole escapade just proved that no matter her manner, Leonde really was just like the rest of them. "As for the goats, well I've seen that before. Where I come from, people that either can't afford horses or have only a small pasturage keep goats and hitch them to carts."

"I wonder why she drove them?"

"I think she must live somewhere far from here that was too far to walk and likely in an isolated spot in the mountains. Enough about her, I wanted to speak with you about Thrad. I'm concerned that Alred is continually leading him astray."

While Brandt was discussing his cat's short-comings, Thomaline was speaking with the guard that had escorted Bulgrid from the council chambers.

"My Queen, the old woman's servant spoke to me when we were retrieving her cart."

"Who was watching her while this happened?"

"No one, My Queen. There was no need. She was standing in the center of the courtyard, and no one approached her while she was there."

Good, thought Thomaline. There was always the risk that Morphas was here in disguise, and she was glad that there had been no contact for Bulgrid.

"What did he tell you?"

"He told me where they lived. It is only the two of them now and he is concerned for his mistress. Because she has no family to visit her now, he says they have few provisions."

Now Thomaline felt somewhat badly about the situation. Bulgrid had made no mention, but it was evident that she was a proud woman and would not have wanted to ask for help.

"Can you put together supplies that they can carry back with them? I think it is a long journey."

"Of course, My Queen. I will attend to it immediately."

"Do so as quickly as you can and catch them before they get too far away. Did the servant tell you anything else?"

"No, but I think he was hoping that someone would check on them from time to time."

"Tell me where they live, and I will let someone know so that we can send out regular supplies." She would have Bulgrid know that the supplies came from Skith. She did not think they would be accepted if it were known that they come from her. She also realized just how perilous the journey must have been for the two old people. The mountain trail they had followed might not have seen danger from other elves, but mountain wildlife was another matter. She called to the guard before he got too far away and made another request. She wanted the old people guarded from danger as they made their way home. As unpleasant as Bulgrid was, she was still her grandfather's relative.

Leonde had gone to her rooms to think. As much as she had never expected nor ever wanted to see Bulgrid again, at least something useful had come from her visit. Mendeth would be furious if he knew that his grandmother had spoken with Thomaline. Leonde hoped that she would have time to counter whatever it was that he planned for the Ward. She needed to speak with her old companions to try and find solutions.

Temor and Skith had returned to one of the small meeting rooms, off the main Council chamber.

"This had been a day for revelations." Temor began.

"Yes, and now I must change my plans." Skith was not happy at that prospect. "I had thought to go some ways with the princess when she leaves tomorrow but now that will be impossible."

Temor could sympathize. There was someone leaving the next day that he too would miss. "I do not think you should entirely change your plans. If you have already told Agretha that you would be going on the first part of the journey, you should. If you do not she might suspect something is amiss, especially after the arrival of our surprise visitor."

Skith thought about what Temor had just said. "You are correct Temor. That would be suspicious. I will go but not too far." He would tell Thomaline of his decision and why he had made it. That decided, he continued on with Temor, "I was more surprised than I could show when that old woman told us of her connection to Leonde and Thomaline. I have never heard of her."

"I was here for the last days of Gendith, and I heard nothing of any surviving family. The banishment must have been earlier and included stripping all mention of them from the records. After meeting her, I can also understand why." Said Temor.

"We can be thankful that it was a short meeting. I cannot imagine what life must have been like for Leonde with Bulgrid in the fortress."

"Be that as it may, we need to devise a strategy for dealing with the various scenarios we have now before us. There are so many of them now. I do agree with Thomaline in that we must deal with Mendeth first." Temor said.

"I know that we should, but I can see a major problem with that. He could be anywhere. I doubt that he will be with the prince and Goldenfell is even larger than it was before." Skith felt his head starting to ache.

"If we engage the prince first, Mendeth may slip through our grasp. He and Morphas might even be able escape Goldenfell."

"If he does, I would welcome the outcome providing Leonde can find a way to lock him out for good. I am sure that even now she will be investigating ways to block out the influence of his blood."

"I wish I knew who this River Lord was and what his part in events might be." Temor had an idea that whoever he was, he must be an elf. There were many that had not come home to Goldenfell when the Call had been sent that had brought many of the adventuring young ones home. He and the others had assumed that most of the missing might have perished. He could not believe that any had stayed away on purpose.

CHAPTER SEVENTEEN

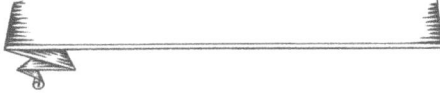

Thomaline and Brandt were on hand to wish the princess well on her journey to her new home. Skith and his guards would ride with them to the first camp and then return the next day. It was a large party that was leaving with Agretha. She had assured everyone in her group that although they would need to build their own dwellings, as it was summer, there would be tents and supplies and plenty of help available to complete construction before winter. Everyone seemed in fine spirits.

"I never thought I would say this, but I really am going to miss her." Said Thomaline to Brandt as they watched the last wagon drive through the gates.

"I'm sure you will see her fairly soon. At least she will be clear of any coming conflict." Brandt reasoned.

"I certainly hope so, but I do wonder if our friendship can survive Cathos." No matter Agretha's brave words, Thomaline had to ponder what would happen if Cathos was dealt with permanently. He was still her brother and worse, he was her twin.

Cathos was on Brandt's mind as well but not regarding his sister. "I suppose that will be up to Cathos."

The next several days saw the arrival of many of Goldenfell's soldiers. The fortress barracks were full and so were the temporary camps that had once again been set up around Goldenfell. The residents of Goldenspire could not help but realize the extent of the danger that was again threatening. Temor and his captains were organizing training exercises for the soldiers and Tallee was doing the same with the Queen's Brigade. Eventually, a decision must be made. Where would Thomaline lead them?

Brandt was again summoned to yet another meeting in the Council chambers. If they ever got the dual threats of Cathos and Mendeth settled, he wanted to seal the chamber doors shut! He hated these interminable meetings! To think that once upon a time he been ordered not to attend.

This time, Temor began the meeting. "We are ready My Lady. We have an army, and they are ready to fight. We just need to know which opponent to engage first."

"Thank you Temor. That question will be answered by the end of this meeting." Thomaline turned to Leonde. It would be her information that would be the deciding factor.

"I have no good news." Leonde looked around the council room. The full Council was in attendance as they had all been advised of the danger posed by both Prince Cathos and Mendeth and his brother. "I cannot make any changes to the Ward that will prevent Mendeth or Morphas from using it for their own purposes." There was an audible gasp from some of the councilors.

Thomaline considered her grandmother's words.

"Have you discovered to what extent they could manipulate the Ward?"

"As to that, I have better news. My companions and I have probed the problem and while we cannot make changes to the Ward, neither can Mendeth. He will, however, be able to continue his use of the portals. It will not take much effort on his part to open and close one. His blood affinity will have seen to that."

"He must have been using the portal where the messages have been discovered." Palin said.

"I do believe he has but I do not know for what purpose." Conceded Leonde. "We have no evidence that the messages were actually made by the River Lord. My examination of them clearly show that they did not come from outside of Goldenfell and the River Lord has never touched them."

"Mendeth created them and using Morphas as the guard who 'discovered' them, made it look like they came from the other side of the barrier." Temor reasoned.

"If he can open a portal, why hasn't he?" Brandt questioned. "Also, would you know if he does? Would the Ward show you?" He did not have a good understanding of the mechanics of how the Ward actually worked. He had never needed to know.

"I should have thought of that." Leonde was chagrined that she had missed examining the Ward for such an occurrence. "I will check as soon as we are finished here. Thomaline, if you have time, could you come with me when I do? I might need your assistance."

"I will try but if he has or has not opened a portal, that still does not tell us what he plans to do." They had so little information regarding Mendeth's plans.

"I suggest that we leave the question of Mendeth for now." Said Skith. "I have revised what I previously thought and now think that Prince Cathos poses a more immediate threat. We cannot sit here idly waiting when there is an army gathered somewhere. We must act."

"Temor, have your scouts found any sign of him yet?" Thomaline asked.

"Unfortunately My Lady, no I have not but I can tell you where he is not and that in turn gives me hope that we will soon learn his location."

"Where do you suspect?" Brandt asked.

"The southern plains. I have bolstered the contingent of soldiers at the portal that has been the center of mystery. I believe that is where we will eventually find Cathos and his army."

"We might not have two separate enemies to deal with after all. We have speculated in the past that they are working together." Thomaline was forming a plan of action now.

"It could be a trap." Brandt declared and then went on to explain. "Cathos could be trying to lure us into one. If we push against his soldiers and then Mendeth opens the portal to reinforcements, we could be outflanked and outnumbered."

"No, I do not think he will do that." Thomaline had been recalling everything she had ever learned about Mendeth. "I do not believe he would have anything to do with Men from outside of Goldenfell. Look how hard he tried to rid Goldenfell of you, Brandt."

"I agree with the Queen, Mendeth's hatred of Men was never faked." Skith vowed.

"Then we must take action. We must move against Prince Cathos. Temor, concentrate your scouts on the route to that portal! We must know if there is any sign of an ambush waiting for us. We can move our soldiers to another staging area along the way while we await news from your scouts. We can go as far as Goldenhollow and wait there." Thomaline's old home fortress was much closer to the southern border and there was room for a large camp around the fortress.

"With you permission My Queen, I will send word to your steward, so he is prepared for your arrival." Skith offered.

"Yes. Do that. Temor, how long will it take to get the soldiers ready to move out?"

"Most of the preparations have been made. We should be able to leave in two days but if I send out scouts now, they will need days more than that before they can reach the southern area and report back."

"How long do think that will take?"

"At least eight days My Lady and they would have to move very swiftly. To do a thorough scout, I would suggest a few days more to add to that estimate."

"We could leave and wait at Goldenhollow." Thomaline proposed.

"What if they have their scouts watching us? They could very well be checking on our movements." Brandt thought. There was still the worry that Morphas could be among them, and he could then report back to his brother what Thomaline was planning.

Thomaline sighed. She was anxious to get their plans in play but now she had to considered what Brandt had said.

"Temor? What do you say?"

"I must concur with Lord Brandt. He has had much experience in battle in his own lands, and I think it would be wise to listen to him. We have been looking for the Skellan, but individuals and even small groups could have hidden from us. We know that they possess great woodcraft."

"Then we will try and do as the Skellan have done. We will send our soldiers off in small groups as well and have them make for my old home of Goldenhollow using various paths. That part of the plan is unchanged. Have the soldiers carry as much of our supplies as they can on horseback. When we leave, we will take the remaining supplies in the wagons with us, although I am sure that Goldenhollow can supply some of what we need."

More plans followed and Brandt found his thoughts drifting from the conversation. Battle plans interested him, not the logistics of getting supplies to where they were needed. When everyone was dismissed he gladly rose and started to follow the councilors until Thomaline issued one more order. There would be another meeting after the evening meal. He could not hold back his groan of disappointment.

On the way back to their rooms, Thomaline forgot about going to Leonde and called for a light meal to be sent before following Brandt and their yaral.

"What will you do after we eat?" Brandt asked when she came in.

"I had thought to ask Master Greth and Master Broday for another training session. I would like to make time each day until we leave for their instruction.

"We shouldn't have food until after." Brandt reminded. "I don't know what their punishment is for spewing our lunch on the practice grounds, and I don't want to!"

"I did not order much, and we can always finish it after we are through."

Brandt did not think he was hungry enough to test the Masters ire. He would wait. He did have another thought he wanted to discuss.

"I don't think I should take Thrad with us when we leave. I think he's too young and he still shies from others."

"How do you propose to keep him here? You are now bonded with him, and he would fret terribly if you left him."

Brandt looked at Thrad as he sat with Alred by the hearth. They both looked as if they were following the conversation. "I will speak with Tallee. He's had the most experience with the bonding and should know what happens when it involves the Queen's Brigade. I will see him before we go for our training sessions."

Brandt was soon disappointed by Tallee's council as he was told that no matter what the outcome, it would be best to have the young yaral with him.

"He is gaining confidence every day and he will try to protect you unto death. Do not leave him behind, My Lord." Tallee encouraged.

When Masters Greth and Broday were consulted they agreed upon a training schedule until Thomaline and Brandt left the fortress with their remaining soldiers. Thankfully, Ilan was on duty when they returned and by the evening meal, there was no evidence of what they had suffered under the watchful eyes of their two instructors.

The evening council was started by Thomaline. "Do you have anything further to tell us Temor?"

The general listed all the preparations that were underway, and he also spoke about some of the contingencies that he had planned based on different possible scenarios when they eventually encountered Prince Cathos and his soldiers.

When Temor had finished his report, it was Leonde who spoke next. "I was testing the Ward this afternoon while you were out," she said to Thomaline, "and I have found something that I did not consciously include in its creation. In one regard, it will not matter if the portals are ever opened by Mendeth; Men will never be able to pass through the barrier, open or not. Only elves. There is also one other fact that I have discovered. That portal has been opened a number of times but only very briefly. None of the others have been tampered with."

"That offers some reassurance even if we do not believe that Mendeth could ever be in league with Men." Thomaline said. She had to wonder why the portal had been opened. Were messages being sent as well as received? Had they been delivered by Morphas?

"But it does bring up something I had considered a few days ago." Said Temor. "If Mendeth is working with someone from outside of Goldenfell, then they must be from Goldenfell." There was a shocked silence created by that statement.

"Explain." Thomaline directed as this was a new wrinkle to consider.

"There are more than a few of our people that never returned after the Call was sent. I am sure that we all thought that those who did not, must have perished during their time in the lands of Men but what if there is one or more that survived? Could Mendeth have made contact with one of our own people when the old Ward failed?"

Thomaline agreed with the reasoning. "It is more than possible. Do not forget that Morphas was a scout, and he was the one that infiltrated a fortress by the river. It was there that he gained information about the Xarlerii. He might have gained more information than he ever told us."

"Yes, but would he have been involved in Mendeth's plotting at that time?" Brandt asked.

"Mendeth had already been removed from the Council by then and from what little we have learned; the two brothers must have been very close even though they kept that hidden. He must have learned something he then passed along to Mendeth."

"I wish now that I had taken the time to learn of their true heritage. These traits of secrecy and treachery must have come from their mother as their father would never have countenanced actions such as those." Leonde was certain.

Gendith's cousin had been nothing like Bulgrid, his mother. Although she also remembered that she knew little of his father.

"Would one of our people really throw in with Mendeth?" Skith questioned.

"He might not know what he is getting involved with. Remember how he tricked the prince when they first met." Said Brandt. "Mendeth is probably using him as well. It now appears that he rarely confided in anyone. I doubt that anyone is safe from his schemes, unless it's his brother Morphas."

"How many never came home?" Thomaline asked. She knew that one of her companions was among the missing. Skith's own son.

"I do not know My Lady." Temor admitted. "Personally, I know of four from here in Goldenspire, but that covers only a small portion of the kingdom. Elves left for hundreds, even a thousand years. There is no way of knowing how many of these perished or even just ignored the call."

Skith was uncomfortable with the discussion. Davos was dead. He knew that his son would never have shirked his duty to return no matter their differences.

"It is useless to speculate further. We must deal with matters as they are. Temor, keep the soldiers moving to plan. Regardless of what Mendeth is doing, we must confront the prince. He has not gathered his army for any good purpose."

"At least he did not get the size of army that I think he might have wanted." Skith told them. "When I rode with the princess as she left, I could see that she had a large contingent of her soldiers with her. She told me that more than a third of their total where now loyal to her and had turned their backs on Cathos. They are tired of fighting battles and want to settle in the lands you have given them. Most do not want to be soldiers anymore. Prince Cathos has less than fourteen hundred with him. With those numbers I do not know what he hopes to accomplish."

"Well that is better news, but he is still treacherous and could do great damage with a force that size. If he can find anything or anyone that he can use to his advantage, he will."

"He has the cunning I'll agree, but he is vain and shallow. Does he have the mind set to take advantage of favorable opportunities? Agretha is the smart one." Brandt gave his opinion.

The meeting drew to a close and Brandt returned to their rooms. Thomaline accompanied Leonde to hers where they spent time discussing what had been said at the day's meetings. Thomaline knew that the battle for Goldenfell lay ahead.

"I must go with our army." Thomaline said and Leonde did not object. She knew only too well the duties of a queen. "I also must leave the kingdom in your hands once again while I am gone. If I do not return, you will rule once more and decide upon a succession plan. I hope that the least I am able to accomplish will be to take all opposition of that rule out of the picture."

"Do you have any suggestions as to whom you would like chosen to succeed me?" She did not want to contemplate that outcome, but Thomaline's input was needed as they faced that reality. She had her own ideas as well.

"I will leave that information for you the day we march. You will also have to decide if the Ward stays the way it is or if it must be changed again."

"I do not have to decide. I cannot change this one. It would require an entirely new one and the construction would depend on what happens after you engage our enemies."

"Then I must be victorious. I do not wish to trouble you too much." Thomaline smiled and then she left to join Brandt. She had his future to consider as well.

Another message had been delivered! It was almost time! He had been gone from Goldenfell for so long and he was tired of hiding who he really was. He had been such a fool by not returning when he had had the chance. His abilities had faded as the many years had passed and glamour had never been one of his best. It would be dangerous to stay now, both for himself and for Goldenfell. He knew that he had dwelt near the river for too long. It was time to leave and move closer to the boundary between this land and his and it was not a short journey. He would go in secret that night!

CHAPTER EIGHTEEN

With most of her soldiers on their way to Goldenhollow, Thomaline was starting to feel at loose ends. Plans had been made and remade with as many contingencies considered as possible and the waiting to take action was making her edgy and again her temper was volatile. The main cause of her current temper was Skith!

"I cannot reason with him! He will not listen, and I doubt he will obey!" She snarled at Brandt as they practiced unarmed fighting tactics against each other while Master Broday looked on.

"For once I agree with him!" Brandt responded while blocking her elbow strike to his head. He soon realized that he should have kept that opinion to himself as he was forced to keep blocking the fists, elbows and feet that were engaged in trying to disable him.

"Well, you should not!" Thomaline was breathing heavily after that flurry of strikes. Master Broday looked on with satisfaction. These two were becoming among the best students he had ever trained.

"Of course, I should!" Brandt responded. It was his turn to attack and hers turn to defend. "It is for your own good and the good of Goldenfell! Your know that!" His anger was rising and would soon be a match for Thomaline's.

"I can take care of myself! I am Queen and I will make the decisions!" Her anger was a distraction and one of Brandt's punches got through her guard and gave her a glancing blow to the cheek. Now that he was becoming as angry as she, he did not even enquire if that punch had hurt. Instead he kept attacking. Master Broday was smiling but he kept pace with the pair, as they had long passed the point simply sparring.

"I know you can! That's not the point. You nearly died last time! What would Goldenfell be without you?" Brandt lashed out once more and his kick caught Thomaline squarely in the chest, knocking her flat on her back on the training ground. "What would I do without you!"

Thomaline lay there, trying to catch her breath. As she did, the anger that had tunneled her vision began to fade. Brandt stood panting in front of her. His anger was still evident. "You will be there and can direct any action, but you still need to consider your own safety." He stated, more calmly than he felt.

"It is my duty and anyway, how can you expect me to watch while you might be killed?"

"It is your duty, but your first duty is to Goldenfell. You're indispensable but I'll promise you this," Brandt offered his hand to help her from the ground, "as much I want to lead the soldiers, I will not do so unless I must. My duty is to protect you." He knew that this was not the end of the argument, merely a pause. Skith was adamant that Thomaline not be directly involved in battle. She had been injured in the fight against the Xarlerii as had Brandt, but Skith was confident that Brandt was replaceable while the Queen was not.

"I will hold you to that promise." Thomaline warned as she dusted off her clothing. "I will try to stay out of harm's way with my Brigade as protection while Temor leads our troops, but you will remain by my side. You nearly died last time as well. We will both sit on our horses in our nice shiny armor and observe."

Brandt did not rise to the sarcasm. "Then we are agreed." Brandt had learned of Thomaline's plan for Leonde and for the future of Goldenfell. If Thomaline was not in a battle, that plan would never be needed.

Master Broday was as pleased as he ever became. For once, he had not cared about the form of the duel he had just witnessed. He had just helped to facilitate the agreement through great physical activity. In his bachelor opinion, fighting hand to hand was a great way to release tension.

"Come," Brandt took Thomaline's hand and started to pull her from the training ground, "you need a bath, and something needs to be done about that bruise on your cheek. The fortress will think I've been beating you!" he laughed.

"Fine! I will speak with Skith." She promised although she hated to think that her councilor had bested her with his stubbornness.

After sessions in the bathing chamber and after assistance from their personal guards for their aid in the healing process the pair went to join the others in the main dining hall for the noon meal. They had barely dipped a spoon into their soup when a soldier quickly entered and asked to speak with General Temor. After a few whispered words, Temor turned to the other diners and ask them for privacy. When the few that had been seated in the hall had left to continue their meal elsewhere, the soldier was then free to report to Thomaline and her advisors. Most of her Council were present and now they could also proceed with their meal. At least that was what Temor had assumed.

"Give us you full report." Temor bade the soldier.

"We have found them, General. The Skellan led by Prince Cathos have been found and are where you thought he must be." The soldier then gave a much more detailed report on the prince's numbers and preparedness. They were well entrenched near the Ward boundary and within striking distance of the portal there. "They appear to have just taken up their position close to the portal otherwise the contingent of our soldiers would have been aware that they were there."

Thomaline left the questioning of the soldier to Temor. She was learning what she needed to know and also, Brandt kept urging her to eat. He was anticipating that they would soon be suffering through another long Council session.

As he had surmised earlier, they were now gathered with the Council to discuss what had been learned from the scout.

"Do you agreed that we can finally move against the prince?" Thomaline asked as she looked around the table. She thought she had been patient long enough.

"Yes, nearly all of our army has gone to Goldenhollow and the need for secrecy has long since passed." General Temor agreed. "Those that have remained here in Goldenspire can leave whenever you say."

"Skith?" Thomaline asked.

"I am prepared as well."

"Then pass the word. We leave for Goldenhollow tomorrow and then we will strike out for where Cathos is encamped."

"What if it's a trap?" Brandt questioned. He already knew what her answer would be, but he wanted to raise the point anyway.

"I am sure he will try something that he thinks will surprise us, but I do not care. We are going." She spoke with grim determination.

"Then we go." Brandt agreed.

The meeting room emptied shortly thereafter. It had not taken long at all.

Thomaline and Leonde gathered together in Leonde's rooms.

"Here is my suggestion for succession. I doubt that you will need to consult it as I have agreed to stay out of the fighting. If at all possible, that is." Thomaline had promised, but situations could change at any time, and she vowed to be ready.

"I am glad that you have seen the sense of that. Will Brandt join you?" her grandmother asked as Leonde had developed a deep fondness for him.

"Yes. That was part of the promise. If I stay safe, so must he. Temor will lead our soldiers as he is their General. I will have the Queen's Brigade for protection and of course, Brandt and Alred will be with me."

It still galled that she had agreed to stay on the sidelines of the conflict. Her fighting blood was rising!

"Be safe." Was Leonde's gentle command.

While Thomaline was with Leonde, Brandt was consulting Tallee regarding Thrad. Tallee was not joining the action. He was deemed too necessary to the ongoing yaral program.

"He is doing much better." Tallee commented as he watched Thrad. The young cat appeared to have grown in just the past few days and now he was confident enough to explore around the fortress on his own, without even Alred for company.

"I had been worried about taking him with me but not now. I think he could be a real asset."

"I know he will, My Lord. I look forward to seeing how your partnership grows." That was his way of saying, be careful and come back.

"We'll be sure to seek your guidance when we return." Brandt smiled as he also considered Tallee to be a friend.

While Temor made the final plans for leaving the next morning, Skith was putting the finishing touches on his own plan. Palin and Haddrim as councilors, were exempt from having to take up arms and join the soldiers, but both had decided to once again don armor and weapons and join the coming fight. Skith believed that there was some grudge against the prince that they would personally like to settle. It might have something to do with their fellow councilor, Sullan. Skith was setting out his own armor. Even though he had gifted the personal armor that his father had created for him to Brandt, he still had another. He had made this one himself. It was not of the quality of his father's, but it was certainly better than average. He had stayed behind during the battle with the Xarlerii, but he was not about to stay in Goldenfell this time. Leonde did not need much help to run the kingdom if it came to that.

"There's only one thing left that I wanted to ask you to do." Brandt said when he and Thomaline finally enjoyed the privacy of their rooms. "I want you to bring Ilan and Staf with us."

"Why? I will have enough guards with the Queen's Brigade."

"I wasn't thinking of them as guards, I was thinking that it could be useful for you to have someone with us that can assist you with your healing abilities. They could be needed and no one else is as compatible with your power as they are."

"I will not ask them to come. They are guards of the fortress, not seasoned soldiers."

"They probably have the same training. I just think that it would be a good idea. That's all."

"If those abilities should be called for, I am sure that there will be enough of our soldiers around to volunteer. No, they will stay in Goldenspire." It would not be necessary to have those two loyal guards accompany them. Thomaline had learned by using her healing ability that she could now sense immediately those that she could draw upon and whom she could not. She would know as soon as she touched a volunteer.

Deciding that further argument was useless, Brandt let the matter drop. Besides, he wanted to finish his inspection of their armor and supplies. The servants had already seen to these items, but he wanted to double check. Their armor was laid out and their newly cleaned weapons had been placed nearby.

"Do you want to add anything to this?" Brandt asked Thomaline as he swept his hand towards the items.

Thomaline went to look over what was there. "Where is my axe? I might need it." Brandt thought she would not, as she was supposed to remain with her Brigade and only observe and maybe direct any skirmishes, but he went to their weapons store to get the item.

When they were both satisfied with their preparations Brandt joined Thomaline where she was seated before their hearth. Their cats had already taken up their spots.

"He has grown." Thomaline observed as she looked towards Thrad.

"Yes, Tallee commented on that as well. He's even taken to exploring the fortress on his own. Whatever trauma he experienced because of Cathos; he now seems to be over it." Sensing that they we speaking about him, Thrad raised his head and looked at them both. He then rose and went to sit and rest his head on Brandt's knee. As he sat with his hand resting on Thrad, Brandt looked at Thomaline and asked, "Do you ever wonder who it might be that's waiting on the other side of boundary?"

"Yes," she admitted, "all the time."

"Do you have any guesses?"

"None. There must have been so many over the long years. When I and my companions left, we scattered once we reached your lands. From the group that left when I did, it was only your grandfather that never returned."

"Tell me about him. Skith refuses to talk about him." Strangely, no one wanted to talk about Davos, not even Palin.

"He was older than me and the rest of my companions. I do not believe he would ever have left on his own if he had not suddenly decided to come with us. Although I never knew what had happened to prompt that decision. He was quiet and thoughtful, and he was no warrior."

"Why would he leave to travel with you? Was it because the rest of you were all trained to fight?"

Thomaline merely shrugged and then said, "Oh, Davos was as well but it did not take with him. I am afraid he was rather hopeless at it."

"That must have pleased his father." Brandt could just picture the displeasure on Skith's face.

"I did not know Skith in those days as I kept away from Goldenspire as much as I could so that Leyrd did not see me, but Davos told me that his father was appalled. As you have learned, Skith was a highly skilled warrior, and you take after him much more than his son. Davos would have been content to become an artist and a poet. He was a thinker and a planner. I now believe he would have been an excellent councilor. He said that his father rejected those pursuits for his son and so when the opportunity presented itself, Davos came away with us. Davos never confided in us but from the little he did say, I think the arguments were fierce and must have come to a head just before we were ready to depart."

"Where did he go?"

"He stayed with us until we crossed from the valley system between this land and yours. We travelled as far as the area of where Lord Silvan's hold was eventually located. Of course, it was not much of a place in those days. One day the others that had ridden with me found that he had left during the night, but we did not tarry long. When he did not return, we did not search for him. I thought he must have turned back. He had hated being on the trail and even though it was dangerous to leave, I knew he regretted coming and wanted to go home. We all went our own ways after he left."

"What do you think happened to him?"

"I have thought about that since I returned and guess that he was killed while trying to return to Goldenfell. This was hundreds of years ago and at that time there were many men in these lands around us and they all knew about elves and that we were here. An elf riding alone would have been an easy target, especially Davos as he had little skill for defending himself."

"Has Temor told you of any of his suspicions?"

"No. As he had said, he only knew of four that had not returned and really, this speculation is useless. If the River Lord is an elf and if Mendeth opens the Ward for him, we will learn his identity. It will not matter who he really is."

Brandt thought it could too matter, but let the matter drop.

"Come, let us go to bed. We could be camping for many days, and I want my comfort while I can, and we will be leaving early tomorrow morning."

Brandt followed her to the bedroom all the while dreading the reason for their upcoming departure. He hated the thought of going to war once more. Even if the outcome would eliminate Cathos from their lives. He also doubted that Thomaline would quietly wait on the sidelines of any battle. No matter what she had promised, she would hardly be able to restrain herself. He would have to find a moment to warn the captain of the Queen's Brigade. He might find guarding his charge more difficult than he imagined.

It was still dark the next morning when Thomaline and Brandt swung up on their restless horses. As always, Thomaline's stallion was pawing the ground, anxious to be racing away, but the horse was in for a disappointment. There would be no racing, only progress as fast as the few wagons that were accompanying them could travel. There were only four left to travel with them as the others had been sent quietly off as had the soldiers. Two of the wagons held medical supplies and healers drove the wagons or rode alongside.

As Temor gave the signal for their departure, another horse was brought from the stables. It was pure black mare with a long flowing mane and tail. Brandt had often admired the horse in the stables but had never been told who the owner was. When Skith emerged from the fortress main doors and took the reins, the mystery was solved but another one remained.

"What are you doing?" Thomaline asked as her horse danced around in circles while keeping its eye on the black horse. The mare snorted and ignored the stallion's antics.

"I am not going to be left behind this time. Leonde does not need me."

"It could become complicated," Brandt warned him, "what if you come up against Cathos? What would you tell Agretha."

"Assuming that I would still be here, I would tell her the truth."

Brandt just shrugged and dug a heel into his horse's side. It was time to go and Skith was certainly old enough to see to his own affairs. He was also wearing armor that looked much like the armor Brandt wore. He had tried to return the gift to his great-grandfather after the battle with the Xarlerii, but Skith had told him that the gift of armor he had made to Brandt could not be returned. He had been saving it for his son and when he failed to come home, Brandt had become the heir to that legacy.

Skith fell into line with Brandt and Thomaline as General Temor led the way. Members of the Queen's guard took up a formation around them and Alred and Thrad paced along beside the horses. Thrad was hesitant at first but soon became used to the pace of the horses and as Alred stayed with Thomaline, he soon kept in step with Brandt and his horse. They were moving with all haste to Goldenhollow and from there, to the southern plains to confront Prince Cathos and if at all possible, Mendeth and his brother Morphas!

CHAPTER NINETEEN

The fighting forces had all joined together at Goldenhollow and after a day of rest, had then moved out, taking the trail that would see them to the southern border. Advance scouts reported back at intervals to the general and for now, the way was clear. They all thought that there was surely a trap of some sort waiting for them.

"Do we move off this path and take another?" Thomaline asked Temor after he had consulted his captains.

"There has been no indication that the prince's soldiers are in the area of our road, but I do not like being confined in this thick forest." He worried.

"I agree with Temor." Said Brandt. "We have little room to maneuver if there is an ambush waiting."

"What do you suggest?" Thomaline looked to both of them for their answers.

"Split up the soldiers." Suggested Brandt.

Temor thought about that for a moment. "We could. This road has many branches. We could have groups take different routes to the south."

"What about when we get there? We might be too spread out." Skith cautioned.

"I think we must send some of your scouts further ahead. We will position more, further along the trails, but we will continue on as we have been. At least for now." Thomaline decided.

"As you say My Lady. I will have them sent to the edge of the forest and out onto the plains. We will locate Prince Cathos and maybe set a trap of our own." Temor said.

Soon, riders and soldiers on foot were being sent to scout for the enemy as commanded.

"Something is wrong." Brandt privately told Thomaline. "There has been no sign of the prince or his soldiers. Surely he's not just sitting out on the plains waiting for us to appear. That makes absolutely no sense and although he's a fool, he's not a complete idiot. He's had experience and has commanded his soldiers in battle for many years. He must have some surprise planned." He concluded once again.

Thomaline agreed. She had spent many hours on the trail, talking with Temor and his captains. They had fought skirmishes with the Skellan before the original Ward had been erected to protect Goldenfell. The Skellan were skilled in trickery, and they had learned that the prince knew how to command his fighting force.

"I do not know the answer." she said. "It could be that he does not want to engage our force here, in the forest. If we do not have room to successfully maneuver, neither would he."

They lay in their tent that night, guarded by members of the Queen's Brigade. Alred and Thrad both had taken to sleeping outside and making patrols around the area on their own. Thomaline had requested that General Temor and Skith place their tents within that same protection as well. They too, were vital to a successful outcome against Cathos.

Brandt's mind had then turned to the problem of Mendeth. He was confident that there was someone on the other side of the Ward and that Mendeth would open the portal. For whom was he planning that entrance? How would this aide Cathos? Brandt did not get much sleep that night.

When they finally reached the beginning of the plains and turned the army to the south, reports began filtering in from the advance scouts. Even though Temor had sent more soldiers to guard the portal closest to their position, Cathos and his soldiers had already fought a winning battle and taken control. Whether the Goldenfell elves had been killed or captured, the scouts could not say. No one had been able to get close enough to find out. Thomaline and Brandt both concluded that Morphas would have had a hand in that.

"He is just sitting there, waiting." Temor explained when Thomaline had called her advisors together.

"We can surround him. He would have no escape if we do battle there." Skith offered.

"That is almost too obvious." Said Temor.

"If he is guarding access to that portal what can he expect to happen?" Thomaline wondered. Why would Cathos need access to the portal? Was he hoping for an alliance with the Men of the land outside of Goldenfell? Did they have Men in the land the Skellan had left or had there only been the Skellan elves and eventually the Xarlerii? Even if he had planned an alliance with Men from the river fortresses, they would not be able to enter Goldenfell through the portal. Did Mendeth know that?

"Leonde said that Men cannot pass through any of our portals. Could he be looking to escape?" Brandt wondered and Thomaline thought he must have picked up on her silent musings. "That would hardly make sense as there is only the land of Men beyond the Ward."

"Is there more than one elf on the other side? Could Mendeth or his brother have made contact with a larger number?" Skith ventured.

Thomaline did not believe that. Even if every elf that was unaccounted for was out there, the number would be too small to help Cathos and Mendeth against her soldiers.

"I do not think so. Remember, there is only Mendeth and maybe his brother that can control the portal. His mind twists and turns and if Cathos trusts what he has been told by Mendeth, then he is an even bigger fool that we thought."

"We are still days away before we get to Cathos and his army. We will camp far enough away to finalize our plans. I have many riders sent ahead so that we will not be caught unawares." Temor ended the discussion. They would continue on as they had been.

The waving green fronds of the prairie grasses were high this season. Rain had been plentiful so far that summer, not hot and dry as it had been when the Xarlerii threatened. Now it was rain that threatened.

"We could do without this development." Brandt offered as he tried to shake off some of the moisture from his cloak before moving further into their tent.

"Temor has sent more soldiers to patrol the perimeter of the camp. He agrees with you. These conditions can hide the enemy's movements."

For the first time in days, Alred and Thrad scratched at the tent, wanting in from the weather. Yaral loved the snow and cold. They could even tolerate the heat of summer, but they hated the continual drenching that they all had experienced over the last two days. The soldier and yaral pairs would suffer with less relief from the rain and the horses, not at all.

Brandt let the cats in and tried to stand far enough away as they also shook the excess moisture from their fur. Thrad looked thoroughly miserable.

"He might be rethinking his bonding." Thomaline laughed until Alred shook again and near to where she sat. He looked a little smug as he lay down and began grooming his fur. Thrad followed suit and soon the smell of wet cat was almost overpowering.

Brandt pick up his cloak and threw Thomaline hers. "Let's go to Skith's tent. We can leave these two here." The cats offered no complaint when they left.

General Temor was already with Skith when they arrived. The general was looking at his map of this Goldenfell area.

"We are here." He pointed out to Thomaline as she and Brandt settled on the camp stools that Skith provided. "We are one day's hard ride from the portal and two if we take our time."

"Well, I know which option I'd chose." Stated Brandt. Speed would be difficult because of the muddy slop that the plains had become.

"Yes. That is what we are planning. We have twice as many soldiers as the prince and I still believe that we can successfully surround his position. He cannot retreat from there. He can only come to us."

"Maybe that is part of his plan." Brandt offered. "Mendeth can open the portal. Men cannot come through, but the Skellan can get out."

"Yes, but what would that gain him? What he wants is here." Thomaline said. The question was met with shrugs.

"How wide are the portals?" Brandt wanted to know. No one had ever spoken about that.

"Big enough for a horse or maybe two people at a time." Thomaline told them. "Certainly not big enough for many to pass through quickly." They could only speculate as the rain continued to fall.

The next day, instead of pushing forward to confront the Skellan elves, Thomaline's army had become stalled. It had been raining heavily for three days now and the plains were awash in water.

"We'll need boats soon." Brandt complained as he returned to their tent. He had been trying to walk about the camp, but Thomaline's tent was on the highest ground while the rest of the area was more than just waterlogged. If this kept up, they would flood soon!

"I know. Everyone is miserable and becoming demoralized. They were prepared to fight not suffer this."

"If I remember correctly you once told me that elves always knew what the weather will do. Is it going to stop soon?" He hopefully asked. His ability to start fires had been welcomed by everyone as the wet wood for their campfires would not light without it, but now he could barely raise smoke with the continuing rain.

"If I sense correctly, it should finally stop during the night."

"Good! It will take days for this grass to dry out enough that we can move swiftly."

"Maybe not that long. Listen! The wind is rising. That should speed things up." Thomaline said.

Brandt was not that heartened as that wind soon began driving the rain hard against the tent and water was being pushed through the tent flaps. The yaral were retreating to the cots. They had had enough of water for now.

Temor too was listening to the wind. He made the swift decision to set out even more guards and moved some of the guard posts further from the camp. He felt sympathy for those that had to obey the order, but someone could attempt a stealthy approach using the howling wind to disguise their movements.

The next morning proved that Thomaline's forecast had been correct. The rain had stopped, and the wind blew the grasses violently about. Everyone still squished around in the mud but at least now there could be a hot meal.

"We will advance tomorrow." Temor decided. "We will make one last stop and then the day after we must be prepared to engage the prince and his forces." The plan was gone over once again as they all still believed that there was some trickery waiting for them by the portal.

"Where shall I be waiting?" Thomaline asked. She did not want to be sidelined during the fight, but she had promised and so had Brandt. Her Brigade captain was not happy to sit out either, but he knew where his first duty lay, and his soldiers had not been too verbal in their complaints. The yaral were just happy that the rain had stopped.

"I am waiting for scouts to return. They will be able to tell us more about the terrain near the portal. I believe there is an area near the portal where I can give you an elevated position where you can see what transpires. You would have the ability to help direct our soldiers if needed."

"I hope that there is such a place." Skith ventured. "If it is as flat as this camp then such a view would be limited."

"If that is what transpires, I will use members of my Brigade to keep me informed. They can take turns bring word of the battle back to us." Thomaline said and then slapped the side of her neck. Something had bitten her!

Soon all of their party were being assaulted by insects. The wind was dying and now after the drenching rain, biting insects were coming out in force. Their armor was no matching for the small invaders.

When the force moved out on the final day everyone was relieved. It had been a miserable two nights as their tents had offered limited protection against the fierce attack of blood-sucking insects. Everyone missed their mountains!

Thomaline tried to cheer those riding closest to her, "At least Cathos and his soldiers would not have fared any better than we."

"Small comfort that is." Brandt had protested. The horses were struggling with the mud and by being bombarded with stinging bites and everyone's temper was fraying. Although that would probably help in the coming battle.

Temor dashed back from the front of their column. "I have had reports and there is a small rise where you should be able to view any battle that we must fight. I have already sent an advance unit so that they will be ready to secure the area. We will stage from there." He said before he turned his horse around to take up his position once again at the fore.

Thomaline became deep in thought. Were they missing something obvious? This was setting up to be a stupid fight. What could be the aim of Cathos?

Brandt's thoughts were alike to those of Thomaline, and a similar uneasiness was making its way through the rest of the soldiers.

The clouds that had darkened the morning, were now moving off and the sun was beginning to peek through. The wind was also picking up and that was driving away most of the insects. At least something was now in their favor. Ahead of their immediate guards, Thomaline could see that their army was starting to deploy on the left side of what looked like a low ridge that spread out a short ways from the portal where the banner of Prince Cathos now flew. He and his men were already in formation and waiting for them.

When Thomaline and Brandt joined Temor and looked down at the army in front of them, the question again arose. What was the prince doing? He had given up what little high ground there was to Thomaline's army, and he was outnumbered. What could he possibly be hoping to gain through this action?

He had ridden hard to reach this spot, and he would have known what he was looking for even if he had not been told. His elven eyes could clearly see a doorway in the barrier before him. He could see no way through it at the moment, but he had been told to be ready to pass through to Goldenfell as soon as it was open. The messages had not specified what he would find on the other side but that did not overly concern him. His only thoughts were about going home!

"Send an emissary." Thomaline instructed Temor. "Ask Cathos if he has terms or if he wants any. I would like to know why he is doing this. Do any of your people know Mendeth or Morphas? If anyone does, send them. If at all possible, I need to know where they are as well."

Temor nodded and sent word for riders to go forward under flag of truce. Within minutes, the prince also appeared to be sending out representatives. When the two small groups met, the discussion was not lengthy. Temor's soldiers suddenly turned about and raced back to the small rise where Thomaline and her advisors sat on their horses.

"Well, what did he say?" she asked when the captain pulled his horse to a stop in front of her.

The captain was at first hesitant but after drawing a calming breath he said, "He was insulting My Queen. His terms are your total surrender, and he wants Lord Brandt turned over to him for treason and execution. He wants nothing else."

Thomaline felt an instant rage but tried to restrain how she felt in the captain's presence. It was not his fault that he had to relay those words.

"What of Mendeth and Morphas?" She asked as calmly as she could.

"It was Morphas that gave me the prince's terms. I think I saw Mendeth at the back of their line, near the portal." As they had thought, Morphas as a soldier and now with a position close to the prince. Mendeth was planning to stay well back and away from the fighting while planning to do something with the portal.

"Thank you captain, return to your soldiers." Thomaline instructed.

"Treason!" Exclaimed Skith. "He must be mad! He must think that he is already King! Treason! Hah!"

Temor was just as incensed but Brandt and Thomaline merely looked at each other. It was obvious that the prince wanted nothing. His 'terms' were all an act.

"General Temor, get your soldiers into formation. We will delay no longer. Let us give Prince Cathos what he does not want!" Thomaline ordered and Temor rode to the front. His captains were with their units and those soldiers were now spread out in a way that enclosed the prince's position, and the lines were three deep. Previously they had agreed to keep the third line back until whatever trap Cathos had to spring was known. Thomaline's position gave her a view of the entire area and was guarded by the whole of the Queen's Brigade which consisted of seventy-five elf and yaral pairs. Brandt sat his horse beside her while Skith had positioned himself on her other side. Alred and Thrad sat in front of their horses. They were all as ready for battle as they would ever be.

The main fighting force would try to engage the prince's army while a small group would have the objective of circling around and fighting their way through to capture or kill Mendeth and secure the portal. Thomaline did not really care which fate befell the traitor. They needed to stop him before he could open the portal and release any unforeseen unpleasantness.

CHAPTER TWENTY

The prince had his soldiers move their horses into a position to oppose Thomaline's force while Cathos remained on his horse to the rear, close to Goldenfell's portal. Observing this, Thomaline had to hope that their strike force would be able to neutralize Mendeth before the portal could be brought into play.

The Skellan army then began to advance, their horses beginning to move at greater speed. General Temor called out to their archers. He wanted to get several volleys away before the enemy was too close.

As Thomaline watched, the first flight of arrows downed a number of the enemy, but the advance continued. After the next flight was launched, Temor had the horns sound, signaling his own charge. The Skellan had not used archers, but as the distance closed, she could see that all their opponents were armed with lances as well as swords. Her own soldiers were at a slight disadvantage until the two armies closed enough as few from Goldenfell used a spear or lance in battle and the Skellan now had a longer reach. As the two groups rushed to battle, the sounds of horse's squealing, the cries of the elves and the clash of weapons was nearly deafening. Price Cathos kept a number of his soldiers back from the main charge. He had other plans for them.

As the battle raged, the area of engagement slowly shifted until the fiercest fighting was to the left of the small rise where Thomaline, Brandt and Skith sat their restless horses. Some of the Queen's Brigade also moved their position, to keep themselves between the fighting and their Queen. Alred and Thrad paced before Thomaline and Brandt. Alred had seen battle before and knew what the turmoil held. He wanted to join the fray, but Thomaline had commanded him to stay. Thrad looked up at Brandt, unsure of what to do. Brandt kept reassuring him and also commanded that the cat stay close. Drawn by the fighting, Skith had now moved away to better observe the battle with a wary eye. His experience in combat was against men not elves. He did not know if he was anxious to join the soldiers or just drawn to the excitement of battle.

With their eyes on the raging fighting, the small group were slow to notice when the prince received a nod from Mendeth that caused him to direct his reserved force of about two hundred to surge forward until a sudden cry of warning rang out. Cathos and his soldiers were charging up the hill towards Thomaline! As soon as they heard the prince and his soldiers begin their charge, Thomaline and Brandt drew their swords and swung their horses to meet the new threat. Her Brigade was now badly out of position and even worse, the trap that they had been expecting was now sprung. The ground just below where they had taken up position was moving as Skellan soldiers were throwing aside the ground cover that had been used to disguise their hiding spots. This was a tactic that the Skellan had used before when Thomaline had first returned to Goldenspire, and she immediately chastised herself that they had not been prepared for this move. When the enemy arose from the shallow pits where they had been concealed to confront Thomaline and Brandt, they were already within the perimeter of the guarding Brigade!

As he stood, anxiously waiting by the portal to his homeland of Goldenfell, he looked one last time at the land that had been his sanctuary. For the most part, he had lived a good life here and there were a few things that he would miss, but nothing could compare to Goldenfell. Soon, something caught his eye, and he turned excitedly to face the portal. Yes! A shimmer was beginning. The way home was opening!

As the soldiers rushed Thomaline's position, Cathos hung back, waiting for his chance. He barely paid attention to the main area of fighting and the fact that his soldiers were losing. They were merely a distraction after all. His real target lay before him!

Mendeth had stayed close to the prince while waiting to spring his surprise. The plan with which he had ensnared the prince had been simple. He had appealed to the prince's blind ambition and conceit and promised him that he would sit on the throne with Thomaline. The prince thought that there was a huge army of Men on the other side of the portal, just waiting for it to open and come to his aid. They were to overwhelm the forces of the Goldenfell elves once the Skellan had done as much damage to that army as possible. Prince

Cathos had had no qualms about the unnecessary slaughter of his soldiers and Mendeth had clearly observed that Thomaline's forces were taking casualties. Mendeth had given the signal to the prince for him to begin his assault on the small group that surrounded the Queen. The prince had given everyone their instructions. The Queen was to suffer no harm, but she was to be taken captive. The prince's primary objective was Brandt. It was also one of Mendeth's. That foul mongrel of a Man would be erased from the land! When that happened, and with no army of Men coming to his aid, Cathos would surely be dispatched by either Thomaline herself or someone from her guard. The only thing that had not gone to plan was the fact that Skith had come along and as he was now with Thomaline, he was in danger. When Cathos rushed away and was unaware that Mendeth had deceived him, the portal was opened, and an elf emerged.

When he passed through the barrier's portal, the sight before him was something he had never imagined. The cries of battle, the screams of the dying elves and horses and the ring of clashing metal was near to overwhelming. What had he been brought home to? There was only one person near the portal, and that person caught his shirt sleeve to bring him away from where he stood. As he watched, the portal was once again closed and the elf who had closed it stood by watching the battle with an evil smile as events unfolded in front of them.

"Who are you? What is happening? Why have you brought me to this?" He could hardly spit out his questions fast enough. He could see that there were two banners to indicate two armies, but they were all elves! Who was Goldenfell fighting?

"All will be revealed shortly. Just stand by an enjoy the view." Was the maniacal response.

There was nothing else he could do, and he watched as a group of what he presumed to be enemy soldiers rushed a small group near Goldenfell's flag that was situated on a low rise above where he stood. Three people on horseback were mostly surrounded by what appeared to be their guards but the riders that had surged forward as he came through the portal were now advancing upon the small party as there was a gap between the guards. Most amazingly those guards had large cats with them! The yaral were also attacking the enemy. As he continued to watch he noticed with amazement, one of the three that had been further from the other two swing his black mare around and rush to join them. One of the others was wearing what looked just like the armor that he remembered Skith had worn at one time and that person was riding a bay horse. That, however, was not Skith. The rider on the black mare had similar armor. It was a shock to realize that this was Skith! That was his father! As Davos turned to look closer at the remaining rider, he could see that he knew that armor as well. It was Thomaline! He would know her armor anywhere. Why was a stranger wearing his father's best armor? He started forward, but was still held back by a grip on his arm.

"My name is Mendeth. Wait here!" he commanded the confused Davos.

Brandt kicked his horse to move in front of Thomaline. He would not let these Skellan harm her! He had no doubt that Cathos was going to try and capture her. Skith drove his mare forward and then he was beside Brandt, waiting to defend his Queen. Thomaline did not want to be defended, and she was trying to maneuver her horse so that she had clear sight of the advancing Skellan soldiers and also to give her a chance to enter the battle. Her guards were out of position and outnumbered, but the Skellan seemed to have forgotten about the yaral. The cats had moved quicker and attacked before their partners had a chance to regroup.

Skith and Brandt sunk their spurs into their horse's sides and surged forward to engage the enemy, but Thomaline was held back by the arrival of some of her Brigade who took up positions in front of her. No matter how she tried to break free of her guards, they kept their formation with their Queen safely in the middle.

"Get out of my way!" she screamed but the guards had strict orders from General Temor and for once, Thomaline's demands were ignored. Frustrated in all her attempts, Thomaline was left with only rising in her stirrups to see what was happening in front of her.

Brandt and Skith, along with members of the Queen's Brigade were fighting furiously, while Prince Cathos had not yet directly engaged with any of Thomaline's protectors. He was looking for an advantage whereby he could get a clean blow at Brandt. Brandt was his only objective. He would deal with Thomaline when the Men that Mendeth had promised, arrived. As he kept behind his soldiers, looking for his opening, Cathos did not at first notice that the army promised by Mendeth consisted of but one lone and very confused elf.

The Skellan forces of Prince Cathos were nearly finished. They had been overwhelmed by the larger numbers of Goldenfell soldiers but the smaller unit that had their sights set on Thomaline were having more success. They were fighting more yaral that soldiers as the Brigade guards had been slower to move. Temor had finally cleared his path of opponents and had looked to the area where Thomaline should have been observing the battle. The danger was now clear, and he called for some of his soldiers to break off from the main engagement and join with him to fight the new threat. Seeing that the general was now bringing soldiers to bear on his position, Cathos looked back to see where his reinforcement were. There were none.

Davos could see that this Mendeth, with his evil smile, seemed to be taunting the leader of the enemy elves. Why was he looking at that other elf like that?

Cathos realized in that moment that he was the one betrayed! There was no army of Men and he and his few remaining soldiers were doomed. His treachery had been rewarded by another's. Mendeth had laid this trap well. Cathos spun his horse and fought his way uphill. He might lose all, but he would do as he had vowed when he set out. Brandt would fall!

Mendeth's gloating had made him blind to his own peril. The squad that had circled around the fighting to reach his position now made their move and fought their way to his position. Horses and soldiers rushed to where he stood and soon the smile was wiped from his face as a sharp sword point was placed against his throat. Davos looked about himself in fear as he was also captured and confined. Had he come home only to find death?

As Temor raced to Thomaline's position, Cathos finally found his chance. Brandt was engaged in fighting two of the Skellan soldiers. Cathos could see what looked like a weak spot on the front of Brandt's armor. A number of sword or lance strikes had damaged some of the links and Cathos raised his lance for the throw. Brandt never saw it coming. He felt the blow and was flung backwards off his horse, the lance lodged in his side.

Thomaline had been watching and now saw with horror the weapon of Cathos strike her Consort. Her scream of anguish alerted her guards, but they were too late as she savagely drove her stallion between them and down to where the fighting still raged.

Cathos had pulled up away from the fight now. He could not contain his laughter. He had bested that insolent disgrace that the Queen had called her Consort. As he looked around at his fallen soldiers he had the scant comfort that if he could not have the Queen, neither would Brandt! His gloating, however, was short lived.

Alred and Thrad had been kept busy, dodging the hooves of the horses of Brigade guard and had never been able to break through to help the other yaral. Their frustration had only been mollified by the presence of their partners. When Brandt had charged forward with Skith, Thrad had been unsure as to what he should do and so chose to remain with Alred. When they had heard Thomaline scream, an opening between guards had appeared in her wake and the cats rushed through the gap. They were too late to stop what Cathos had done, but they were not too late to stop Cathos. Alred did not hesitate as he charged the prince's position.

His attention elsewhere, Cathos was barely aware of the large grey shape that knocked him from his horse. Alred had sprung with practiced ease at his target and the prince fell sideways from his saddle. Before he could use his sword or pull his dagger from its sheath, another grey shape appeared above him while the first held him down. Through his bond with Brandt, Thrad could feel the mortal wound of his partner and wasted little time in dispatching the one who had injured him just after he had arrived in Goldenspire. Alred released his hold on the now dead elf and seemed to momentarily smile before they both rushed to the still ongoing fight.

When Thomaline burst onto the scene, she immediately engaged those that were fighting around Brandt's downed figure. Skith soon joined her as well as Alred and Thrad, although Thrad was not fighting. He had leaped through the soldiers and was now crouched beside Brandt, snarling at anyone who got too close. Those that did felt his fangs and claws whether they belonged to Goldenfell or were Skellan.

The minutes stretched on but eventually, the few remaining Skellan soldiers soon realized that they had no reinforcements and then saw that their prince was dead. It was over. They were finished. Their numbers were few when they finally threw down their weapons and were marched away from the battlefields and held as prisoners.

Thomaline threw herself from her saddle and removed her helm as she ran to were Brandt had fallen. Precious moments were lost while she worked to sooth Thrad so that he would let her see to Brandt. Was her Consort even alive?

Skith sat his horse, his chest heaving with the effort spent in battle. He was watching Thomaline run to Brant when his attention was drawn away by something else. He could see that the soldiers that had been tasked with apprehending Mendeth had completed their mission. Skith could not help Brandt now, but he vowed he would see to Mendeth.

Mendeth was keeping very still. He did not doubt that the slightest movement on his part would lead to death. That was until he saw Skith remove his helmet as he rode to where Mendeth was being held.

Before Skith could speak, Mendeth asked, "Have you seen Morphas? Is he safe?"

Skith coldly looked at his former councilor and ally before he turned his head to the area of where the prince lay. He could clearly see a figure lying on the ground nearby, a sword wound to his neck. Morphas was no longer a threat.

"He is dead." Skith's voice was glacial.

Mendeth hung his head for moments and then raised his eyes to Skith.

"We did what we set out to do. He would have been proud of that." Said Mendeth.

"And what was that? What was all this death in aide of?" Skith demanded.

"We have rid Goldenfell of that usurper, Brandt, and eliminated the threat brought by the prince of the Skellan. Thomaline is now free to choose someone worthy to be by her side and it will not be that idiot prince. I have brought someone back to Goldenfell that you will be proud to see stand beside a queen." Mendeth thought that Skith would more than approve of his candidate for consort.

"The prince might not have had such lofty ambitions if you had not given him the idea in the first place." Skith sneered. "As to someone worthy of Thomaline, well then you know nothing. No one will ever be as worthy as my great-grandson Brandt, no matter who you have brought through the portal!"

Skith was done with Mendeth. Temor had now joined them and as they looked at each other, they came to the mutual decision. They did not need the Queen's permission to meet out the punishment. Skith's sudden swing of his sword met no resistance. Mendeth was dead! As the body toppled to the ground, Skith became aware of another prisoner who had been held further back and out of sight. When the guards dragged the struggling figure forward, he could hardly believe his eyes!

"Hello father." Davos began fearfully. He had just witnessed what had happened to that Mendeth person and was unsure what his father would do to him. He was trying to be brave.

"Davos? How are you here? I thought you must be dead!" Skith was amazed. He had thought that his only son was lost forever. "You!" he exclaimed as another thought pushed its way into his mind. "You are the River Lord! It is you that has been sending the messages!"

"No father. I am the one who has been receiving messages. I thought that Thomaline needed me and was calling me home." Was the quiet reply of Davos.

Skith dismounted and strode to his son, who he suddenly gathered into a bearhug, and he was near to tears as Davos already was. Then Davos started to explain all that had happened and Skith began to understand to total betrayal that Mendeth had visited upon everyone.

Temor moved his horse forward and made Skith aware of what was happening further up the slope. Brandt was dying.

"He is still alive, but not for long I am afraid. You need to go to him. Now." Temor told Skith who then clutched his son's arm and dragged him to where Brandt lay while Thomaline attempted to tend his wound.

"Thomaline, what can we do?"

"I can heal him! I just need the right person to help me!" She exclaimed as she pushed a piece of cloth against the ragged hole in Brandt's side. She had managed to pull the lance from his body but now the blood ran from the wound. Two of her soldiers lay collapsed nearby and she quickly explained that she could save him if she found someone whose magic would work with hers. She had a healing power that most did not comprehend.

"Why did I not listen to him? I should have brought Ilan with us." Thomaline lamented before frantically calling to more of her soldiers. As she reached for them in turn, she could instantly tell if they could help her or not. So far only two had contained what she needed. She had slowed the bleeding of Brandt's wound but that was all. She caught another hand and successfully used that life force to heal the wound a little more. The blood merely trickled now but that was only a small part of the problem. The wound was deep inside, and she had only done such a complicated healing once before. She needed someone much more compatible!

Skith meanwhile was trying to explain to his son what was happening.

"My grandson? I have a grandson. Are you sure?" Davos asked in amazement.

CHAPTER TWENTY-ONE

While Davos questioned his father regarding the parentage of the person on the ground, Temor went to kneel by Brandt's head. There he gently worked off the helmet and Brandt's ashen face was exposed.

"That really is my grandson! Why, he looks just like Elthea and her father!"

Thomaline had been ignoring Skith and his son while she laid a hand on soldier after soldier. No one was compatible!

"Here, take my hand," Skith insisted, "we are family so that might work in this instance."

Thomaline did not waste time with words, she merely took the hand that was offered to her. Immediately, she could feel the power rise and Brandt's wound closed. At least on the surface.

"Not enough! Skith, it is not enough!" Skith was wavering and Temor rushed to support him before he fell.

Davos had been watching, still in awe that the dark-haired man lying on the ground so grievously wounded, was indeed his grandson.

"Thomaline. What are you doing? How did my father help you?"

For the first time, Thomaline actually noticed who was standing before her. She was amazed to see her old companion, but she had no patience for his questions.

"I can heal him. I have the power, but he is so badly hurt that I am afraid I might draw more than others can give to complete the process." She swiftly explained.

"If my father has helped then try me as well. I can see that we share a greater percentage of blood." Davos then reached out his hand to Thomaline.

Marveling at his return, Thomaline nevertheless took the hand that was offered. With a gasp, she felt another surge of power. This was much more than she was used to dealing with. Davos was more than compatible with her; he was also a match for Brandt.

"Who is this man to you?" Davos asked as he knelt by the unconscious form.

"He is my Consort and the love of my life. I have to help him Davos. I cannot lose him!" She looked desperately into his eyes.

"Then take what you need." Davos was not afraid although he should have been.

Thomaline closed her eyes and concentrated as hard as she could to feel the internal damage before beginning to pour a healing essence into Brandt's body, transferred from Davos.

Davos could feel the drain start and gasped in surprise. Maybe he should have been afraid.

While Thomaline worked, Thrad pushed his way back through the mass of bodies that stood watching the Queen work her magic until he was near Brandt once more. Already Brandt was beginning to have better color in his face and his breathing was not as shallow.

"Thomaline! You must stop! You could kill Davos!" Skith warned as he pushed his way free of Temor and crawled to hold his son in his arms.

Thomaline stopped the transfer but kept her grasp on Davos' hand.

"Have you done it?" Temor hoarsely asked. He feared for Thomaline if Brandt died.

"No. Not all of it. There is still bleeding inside and if I do not stop that, he will still die."

"Then take all you need. I think that I have been badly manipulated and the result is this carnage you see around us. With this, I can atone. Do it!" Davos commanded, his voice stronger and stern.

"No! You cannot! You cannot take one life to save another." Skith was adamant that he would not lose his son now!

"I have to act. I cannot wait." She told them and then she started the healing process once more and again Davos felt the drain on his body.

"Take me! Use me as well!" Skith commanded and reached to place his hand on the hands of the others.

Davos continued to feel the drain, but it was now less than it had been. His father was making a difference.

Thomaline could feel the torn body under her hand healing the final damage and now she slowed the transfer of energy to a trickle as both Davos and Skith looked ready to collapse. She would have to draw from herself to complete the healing or Davos and his father would die. When she released their hands. Temor and a soldier quickly caught them and moved to lay them on the ground near Brandt.

As Thomaline prepared to attempt the last of the required healing, both Alred and Thrad pushed against her and Brandt. Without using conscious thought, she reached inside herself to gather enough power to complete the healing until she felt another power. A pair of powers. The yaral could bolster her ability, and did.

Brandt slowly came to the realization that he was lying on the ground, looking up at the blue and cloudless sky over head. What had happened? For the moment, he chose not to think about that, and he realized that he did not want to move. He knew it would hurt. He had been wounded! It was slowly coming back to him. He had been engaged in a fight with two enemy soldiers before something had dealt him a horrendous blow that knocked him from his horse. After that, things had blurred until it had all gone black. Where was he? Where was Thomaline?

Alred had gone to nuzzle Thomaline. She was awake but not moving.

Thrad crawled over Brandt and licked his face, leaving a roughened patch of skin and beard where his tongue had been. Brandt hated it when a cat licked him, but he was oddly comforted by the yaral's attention. Thrad lay as close as he could alongside Brandt's body while placing his head on Brandt's chest.

"My Lord. My Lord, can you hear me?"

That was Temor. Why did he sound so concerned?

"My Lord?"

"Yes Temor, I can hear you. Where are you?" Brandt did not want to move his head to see where Temor was.

Temor left Skith's side and bent near Brandt. "I am here."

With great effort, Brandt raised his arm slightly for Temor's assistance, "Help me. I want to move, but I don't think I can do that by myself. Where is Thomaline?"

"Here. I am here." Thomaline's voice was faint, but she was responding gladly to Brandt's voice. "Temor! Do not let him move. He must stay still."

"Why? What's wrong with me?" Brandt asked, but did as he was told. He had decided that he really did not want to move after all and now realized that any attempt to get up was far beyond him.

Thomaline crawled to him, "You were mortally wounded, Brandt. I healed everything as well as I could, but I am afraid something might tear open if you move around. We will get a litter for you." She said as she tenderly stroked his cheek.

"I hate litters. They sway about and make me feel sick."

"I know. I know, but you will have to endure it. I do not think I can heal you anymore than I have."

If he was healed, why did he feel so bad? "Alright then. Do as you must. I think I need a nap anyway." He said and then closed his eyes.

One of her guards helped Thomaline to her feet where she swayed a little but soon managed to steady herself when Alred pressed against her legs. When she had, she saw Skith and Davos also lying on the ground a few feet from Brandt.

"Will they be all right?" She asked as one of the fortress healers knelt, assessing them both.

"I do not know My Queen. I have never seen anything like this. We must get them back to Goldenspire. With help, we might be able to do something."

Temor now stood and joined Thomaline as she looked around the field of battle. Bodies were everywhere. Most of the Skellan were dead but many of her own soldiers also lay among the dead and dying and here and there the body of a fallen yaral also lay.

"Where are traitors? And where is Prince Cathos?" Her anger now surged.

"They are dead Thomaline." Temor quietly said. "Morphas fell in the attempt to take you and kill Brandt. It was the prince that threw the lance that pierced Brandt but your yaral got their revenge. Alred and Thrad killed him. Mendeth is also dead but that was Skith's doing." Temor felt numb as he relayed what had happened.

"What an absolute waste." She said before ordering a litter for Brandt and calling for the wagons and healers to be brought to help treat and move the wounded; Goldenfell's and the Skellan alike would all receive equal care. Those that lived would return to Goldenspire, the rest were to be buried in this field.

A bitter monument to blind greed and stupid ambition. It would be a warning against treachery as well.

EPILOGUE

Brant lay in their bed, finally feeling like he was on the mend. It had been a long and slow journey from the battlefield near the southern portal. He did not know which was worse, travelling in a litter or a wagon. One was rough and jolting while the other swayed along, keeping his stomach in constant turmoil. Now at least, his bed was still. He understood from Thomaline that his wound was healed but his actual recovery would take time.

Thomaline had set out directly from the battle with a wagon and the litter. She was determined to get Brandt, Skith and Davos back to Goldenspire as soon as possible. She was adamant that the pair's sacrifice would not result in their deaths. Davos was in the greatest need. On the trail home, she had bolstered the strength of both father and son as much as she could but the energy of the soldiers that assisted her offered small recompense for what she had taken from the pair. She desperately hoped that Ilan and Staf could help her repair the damage she had caused. Temor remained behind to oversee the tending of the rest of the wounded and the burying of the dead.

When Thomaline reached Goldenspire, Leonde was there to greet her. She was the one to send for Thomaline's guards as Skith and Davos were taken to the infirmary while Brandt was taken to the royal apartment. When Ilan and Stef had arrived Thomaline managed to stabilize both Skith and Davos but that was all she was able to do. She desperately need to rest, and Ilan an Staf needed to recover. Skith and Davos had indeed been close to death.

Two days later, Thomaline tried once again to help her councilor and his son. Skith was restored to almost full health, but Davos had a different result.

"I have done my best Davos, but I am sorry that it is not enough. I am afraid that I took too much, trying to heal Brandt."

"I do not blame you, Thomaline. I blame myself. If I had come back as I should, this would never have happened. You only did as I told you. I would have given all to save him."

"You did not understand the consequences of your actions. None of us knew what would happen." She then tried to explain his condition. "I believe you will recover but not to the extent that your father has. I am sorry to say that I have stripped years from your life." How many years was unclear.

"At least I still have a life. It will also be a life I can live here in Goldenfell."

Davos should have had thousands of years to look forward to but that was not what she felt. Thomaline believed that his life span had been halved or maybe even more than that had been taken to save Brandt's life.

"When do you think I can leave this place?" Davos asked. His father had been released days earlier.

"I have spoken with the other healers, and they agree that you can leave here, but you will be taken to a room in the fortress near your father. You will need to rest as much as you can for a while." Maybe a long while. Davos was still weak.

Skith came to the infirmary that day and with the help of servants, moved Davos to his new quarters.

When Thomaline had been able to see Leonde, she had been given two pieces of news. The first was that Leonde had learned how to close the portals once and for all. She just needed Thomaline to approve that move.

"Yes! Do so as soon as possible. If I had not wanted to see what was happening outside of Goldenfell, Mendeth would never have been able to trick the prince into his foolish scheme or taken advantage of Davos' desire to return home. Close them before some other unknown distant relative arrives on the scene. Goldenfell will remain a hidden kingdom!"

The second bit of news was that Agretha was on her way to Goldenspire.

When the princess arrived, Thomaline was waiting for her at the gate. She could immediately tell that Agretha had learned the fate of her twin brother.

"I know that you did what you had to do. Cathos was a fool." Agretha sadly told her. "I have come to learn what has happened to my soldiers."

Thomaline guided Agretha to the infirmary that held the wounded Skellan and to the barracks were the remainder of the Skellan soldiers were being held.

"Stay as long as you need, Agretha. When the wounded can ride, you can take them and the others with you when you return to Pellisgould, but you will always be welcome to return to Goldenspire."

Although neither Skith nor Agretha said anything to her, Thomaline could see that whatever had previously developed between them had now cooled. Skith would not be making journeys to Pellisgould, at least not for a while. Maybe when Agretha had a chance to work through her grief at the loss of so many Skellan soldiers and her brother, they would have a chance at a future together.

Leonde closed the portals but not before expanding the boundaries one more time. Goldenfell was now much larger than in the past. When that was accomplished, she informed Thomaline that she was leaving. Leonde wanted to return to her quiet life in her cottage.

"I will have my servants and my guards. I long for quieter times once more. Come and see me when you can." She said to Thomaline before she left.

The day that Agretha left with her Skellan soldiers, Brandt was released from the confines of his bed. His first stop outside their rooms was to see Davos. Skith was already there and Thomaline entered the rooms shortly after Brandt.

"Hello." Brandt said to the strange elf who was sitting beside the small fire in the hearth.

"Hello." Davos replied as he hungrily looked at the man who was his grandson. "You look like your grandmother and her father, Thedrie."

Brandt was not quite sure how to take that comment. "Thank you. I think."

Davos smiled, "Now that I know who you are, I think that I would have known you anywhere."

"Tell me about them." Brandt requested. And Davos did.

Davos told them about his life after he had left Thomaline and her companions. He had travelled far but his was not the life of a warrior. He had been a bard and a poet and from time to time he had worked in the forges of smiths and armorers but his was an artistic talent. He did not make many tools or weapons, he made art. He had some of his father's talent and that had been a useful skill over the years. He had constantly moved from place to place, and kept mostly to himself as his glamour ability was very small and his lack of aging necessitated his constant movement to new areas. He had to keep his ears hidden, but he could manage to disguise his eyes. Those he could make human-like.

One day he had approached a small village smithy, looking for work. He had been taken in by the family and here he had met Elthea. He had fallen hopelessly in love. He had never felt love before. He knew that it was wrong to stay and marry, but he could not leave her. They had a son, and Davos had stayed for as long as he could, but in the end he had to leave. The villagers had been starting to make comments regarding his appearance by the time his son was five years old. He had lived there too long and now Elthea, who had been a young bride, was looking older than Davos. His remaining would have put their lives at risk as well as his own. One night he had quietly left their cottage and laid a false trail at the nearby river, faking his death. He never went back to that area again. It would have hurt too much. Instead, he managed to work up the courage he needed, and he had started to make his way back to Goldenfell. Unfortunately, he had been side-tracked from that goal before he reached the river Havers. He had spent the remaining years moving as often as he needed before finally taking control and leading the Men of the river. The River Lord had been born.

"Why did you not return when the Call was sent?" Skith asked Davos.

"I was afraid. I was afraid to see the disappointment in your eyes when I told you of the life I had led. I fear that I was always a disappointment to you."

"No Davos. That is not correct. I now realize that it was I who was the disappointment. As many fathers do, I made the mistake of trying to make you in my image, rather than letting you lead the life you needed. I am sorry that my actions kept you from your home." Skith believed that it was his actions that had resulted in Davos' current condition.

The two would need to spend time to sort through all their issues, but Thomaline felt confident of the outcome.

The last question to be answered was about how Davos had come into contact with Mendeth.

"It was over two years ago." Davos explained. "One night I was walking the fortress ramparts when I noticed someone sneaking about, outside the walls. I had lived with Men a long time, but I still have elven eyesight, and I knew what he was and then he saw me too. When I went to him, he explained that he was on a mission for the Queen of Goldenfell and that you needed information on the Xarlerii. When he left, I followed. That was when I discovered the barrier that had been created by your old Ward. That had been the first time I had gone that far north of the river, but I could not cross the barrier. I made regular trips afterwards, but I was not there when the Wards were changed and knew that I had missed a chance to return. I could still see the new boundary, but it was now closer to the river. Not too long after that, I found the first message. It told me that the Queen needed my help." The rest was easy to unravel. Mendeth had played everyone false and for fools.

Brandt learned about his ancestor and was happy to call Davos "grandfather," even though Brandt looked the older of the two.

Fall was ending and winter approaching when Brandt and Thomaline went to the stables to collect their horses. Now that he had fully recovered from his wound, they were riding to see Leonde.

"Have you heard from Agretha lately?" Brandt asked. Thomaline and Agretha had been in regular contact since Agretha had left with the remnants of the Skellan soldiers, but there had not yet been any visits.

"Yes. She tells me that most of the accommodations have been constructed and that they are well set for winter, although some might need to share living arrangements until next year. I have assured them that if needed, we will still send supplies."

Brandt hoped that despite Cathos and his actions, the two women would be able to continue to grow their friendship.

"Did you ever get a reply from Bulgrid?" Brandt knew that while he had been recovering, Thomaline had sent word to the old woman, informing her of the fate of her grandsons.

"I did, but it was not repeatable, even though you were mentioned several times, just not favorably. She did not, however, return the supplies I sent to her." With Mendeth and Morphas dead, Thomaline had taken on the responsibility of seeing that Bulgrid and her old servant did not starve to death in their mountain hideaway.

"So everything and everyone is being looked after and this is as normal as it gets?" Brandt laughed.

"There is only one item left to deal with, and I have scheduled that for the next council meeting."

Brandt groaned. He had to find a way to keep those damn meetings to a minimum. "What is it now?'

"I am tired of having a Consort." She told him and then laughed at his horrified look.

"What have I done? Are you replacing me? Why?" Brandt was truly shocked.

"Yes, that is it," Thomaline laughed again, "I am replacing you with a prince."

Brandt mind raced. Prince? What Prince? There was no prince. Who had usurped him?

"Prince Brandt!" Thomaline shouted over her shoulder as she dug into her horse's sides with her heels.

Brandt sat for a few moments until he too was laughing and then the soon to be Prince Brandt raced up the mountain trail after his Queen.

$$\times$$

the end

Books By Laurie Cook

The Goldenfell Saga:
AN ELF'S HOMECOMING – Book 1
TROUBLE IN THE LAND – Book 2
THE GHOSTLY GUARDIAN
IS SOMEONE WATCHING
A LINGERING EVIL
NEARLY DEPARTED
A CONSEQUENCE OF WAR

I hope you enjoyed the book.
THANK YOU

www.ingramcontent.com/pod-product-compliance
Ingram Content Group UK Ltd.
Pitfield, Milton Keynes, MK11 3LW, UK
UKHW022148300125
454444UK00010B/268

9 798230 438595